MARY DOVE

BOOKS BY JANE GILMORE RUSHING

Mary Dove
Tamzen
Against the Moon
Walnut Grove

Doubleday & Company, Inc.
Garden City, New York 1974

All of the characters in this book are fictitious, and any resemblance to actual persons, living or dead, is purely coincidental.

ISBN: 0-385-08302-5
Library of Congress Catalog Card Number 73–9029

Printed in the United States of America
FIRST EDITION

TO JAY (ALL THINGS, ALL PLACES)

The world was all before them, where to choose
Their place of rest, and providence their guide:
They hand in hand with wandering steps and slow,
Through Eden took their solitary way.

PARADISE LOST, BOOK XII

PROLOGUE

In the time of a strange withered spring, a lone cowboy rode through country where scattered little flat-topped hills rose sharply above a rolling terrain watered by narrow running streams. He stayed, when he could, on the high places, so nothing got between him and the great clean sky and he could look across the desolate browned land to rest his eyes on the purple horizon.

Larks sang all around him, each lifting call a fresh surprise for there were few other signs of spring. Tender leaves of willow, clouds of blossoming plum, thrusting, juicy grass blades—almost everything alive—had been blighted or cut down by an incredible late blizzard. Up where he rode, the cowboy could almost forget how near spring had been five days before, when freezing mist came suddenly filling the sky, coating everything with ice before it turned into heavy, blasting snow.

Wheeling birds in the sky were a dark reminder. The

cowboy's job was down among the creeks and hollows, where piles of dead and stinking cattle lay, victims of that unseasonable storm. He had already convinced himself that there were no Bar Diamond cows left alive on that range, but here and there he had found new little calves, that must have been sheltered somehow by their mothers' bodies, bawling pitifully. There was nothing to do about these calves but shoot them. He thought the boss might have said even that was a waste of ammunition, but he hated to leave them to starve or be killed by the wolves.

He was about through. He was ready to leave early the next morning for the Bar Diamond headquarters on the Stakéd Plains, a hundred miles away, but he figured he ought to check this Spring Creek country before he quit. The cows ranged this far sometimes, and they had run scared in that storm—there was no telling where they had got to. The boss would want a full report.

A creek ran just below him. He could ride to the edge of a steep bluff that rose above it, at a place where it widened out and curved. He dreaded to go and look down, for if there was anything there to see he guessed he knew what it was. Still, he would have to find out. He thought he would not ride any farther, but would call the job done at this point. So he stopped stalling, and rode to the edge and looked down.

He had never seen anything like what lay below that bluff. He had seen piles of cows, but when he first looked at this mass of dirty-looking grayish colored stuff damming up the creek he could not think what it was.

Then "Sheep," he said. Lord knew how many sheep. All that fellow Pardue had, for sure. He could imagine how mist and snow had gone through their wool—they must have been blocks of ice before the thaw set in. He had seen the herd feeding on hillsides sometimes, but he never would have thought it could make such a mountain of soggy wool. He felt sorry for Pardue—this must have been everything he had in the world.

At the edge of this sodden mass that had been a herd of sheep, something separate lay. The cowboy became aware of it that way—a dark, separate body. When he realized he was deliberately not letting his eyes focus on it, he made himself look, made his mind take in what it was. A black horse. Saddled.

Then he knew he could not ride away from that scene without first going down into the creek bed. He rode a little way, to where a gentle slope led to the water. In spite of snow water flooding everywhere, the creek here had not risen much because of the dam formed by the sheep. He could have ridden his horse along the creek bed but dismounted and left him because he was acting up either at the stink or at the sight of the dead animals.

He paused near the black horse. He thought he knew what horse that was; it wouldn't be hard to guess what had happened to its rider.

Here at the bend in the creek, the water ran right up against the rock bluff, but there was a dry ledge where a man could walk. The ledge made a narrow, irregular path. Some places, it was heavily shadowed by rock jutting out overhead. In bad weather it would make a pretty good shelter for an animal or a man.

But not good enough. The cowboy knew now what he had to find next and could say that to himself. He moved slowly, not wanting to find it.

It was lying up against the rock in deep shade, so the cowboy had to come clear to it before he knew for sure. It was soaked, shapeless, gnawed at. But he knew.

"Good God," he said, and turned away sick.

During the two seasons the cowboy had been at the Badger Creek camp, he had seen the man Pardue three or four times. For a sheepherder he seemed like a pretty good fellow, though kind of peculiar too. He lived by himself—so he told the cowboy once—in a dugout over in the hills a piece, at the head of some creek he didn't know a name for. The cowboy had never seen the place. Though they had talked together by the fire at the cow camp, Pardue never told exactly where he lived or offered any sign of wanting company there. No telling where he had come from, or why.

Even so, he had to be buried. The cowboy went and got a slicker that he kept rolled up behind his saddle, and he wrapped the remains in it and carried them up out of the creek to the top of a little rise. Then he rode back to camp and got a shovel, and it took him nearly the rest of the day to do the burying. At the last he moved a large flat stone to the head of the grave. If it hadn't been so late he might have tried to cut a name on it, but he didn't reckon there would be anybody to read it if he did.

"God help you, Pardue," he said, and rode off.

He hated to leave the grave. He didn't know whether he would ever come back to this range or not, whether the boss would ever want to run cows there any more. He might never see that grave again. His might be the only eyes that ever looked upon it, with the knowledge of what it was and who lay buried there.

He turned back once and called, "Goodbye, old hoss."

Then, out on higher ground where the light was still good and the land was open, he ran his pony hard, getting away from there.

Now this was nearly a hundred years ago, on the Rolling Plains of Texas, and men who brought beasts there to feed on the grass of the open range lived solitary lives.

I
Mary Dove

On the morning the icy mist blew in, the father and daughter were getting their corn patch ready for planting. When they saw the streak across the north, the man said he reckoned they were in for some weather and might not get to plant as soon as they thought. As the dark blue moved up the sky, a chilly wind came out of it and the girl went in and got coats, but they kept on digging. Even when the first fine mist touched their faces, they could not have guessed what weather was to come.

"Late for a cold spell," the father said, "but we better get some wood in, just in case."

They said to each other that they hoped it wouldn't be a hard freeze. They had seen late cold spells before and knew how early leaves and blossoms could be killed–summer delayed–the wild fruit denied them. Such a freeze would be a disappointment.

They piled wood on the loose rock floor under the brush

arbor that the man had built in front of the dugout, protecting the entrance, making a place almost as good as an extra room. Wood kept dry there, and was handy.

While they worked, they noticed that the birds had disappeared, their songs hushed. A half-tame young cottontail that the girl had been petting came and crouched behind the woodpile, not minding their presence, and the chickens gathered together, restless, under their roosting trees. The old cow bawled, and sheep bleated anxiously from some place not far away.

"Sheep's silly," the man often said. "They get worked up too easy."

He took care of them though. He said he would take old Shep in a little while and go see if they would be better off in a more sheltered place.

The man and girl finished bringing in under the arbor all the wood they had cut, and they carried several armloads down into the dugout. The sky was thickening, lowering, and the wind kept blowing harder all the time.

"It's gonna get colder than I figured," the man said. "I got to go see to them sheep."

"You want me to help you, Papa?" the girl asked.

"No," he said slowly, considering. "No, Mary Dove, I tell you, you better stay here and milk. Milk early, and shut up the calf with the cow. Might keep it from freezing."

They had a partial dugout in the hillside with a brush roof over it to shelter the cow. A pole fence built out from it made a pen to keep the cow in when they needed to. When Mary Dove got through milking she shut the cow and calf up in that pen.

Going back to the dugout with the bucket of milk, she was surprised to see her father returning already. Maybe he had decided there was no use in trying to move the sheep, she thought, then saw he carried a lamb under each arm. She put the bucket on a bench by the door and went to meet him.

"There's some mighty little lambs out there," he said. "I'as a-feared these here twins might not make it through the night."

"Oh give them to me, Papa," she said, reaching out to him. "Let me take 'em in out of the cold."

"I'll take 'em," he said, "while you see about your milk. You can go back with me then, for there's a few more fresh borned that we might as well save if we can. If any comes in the night, I reckon we've just lost 'em."

It was still not very cold in the dugout. Like the cow shelter, it was partly dug into the hillside, but it was deeper, and the roof was covered over with earth. Both summer heat and winter cold took a long time getting into their snug house.

The man laid the lambs on a sheepskin in one corner. "They'll be all right," he said. "We'll get the rest before we stop to build a fire."

Mary Dove had been about to go and rinse her strainer rag at the spring, but seeing the need for hurry she said, "I'm ready, Papa."

They noticed how ice was forming on everything, coating each leaf and twig of every bush and tree, but began to run without thinking how the grass under their feet must be. Almost at once the man slipped and fell down. Mary Dove stopped and turned to him anxiously, but he got up easily and said he wasn't hurt.

"We better be careful though," he said. "You have to remember haste makes waste, a time like this."

It was about a quarter of a mile to where the sheep were. Their bleating filled the air like cries of frightened children, while the man and girl hurried to them as fast as they could. They were bunched in a shallow little hollow, moving ceaselessly, bumping into each other, going nowhere, crying and crying. The couple pushed through them as best they could, hunting new lambs. When they picked one up, they could feel ice crusted on its wool, but the bodies were beating and warm. At last they were carrying five lambs. They paused over a dead one.

"Tromped on, I reckon," the man said.

Mary Dove bent to it briefly. "Poor little thing," she said, but knew they must move on. Dark was coming fast, and the cold pierced clear through her.

"We better take these here uns in," her father said. "We couldn't manage any more if we found 'em."

He carried three, and Mary Dove carried two.

"We'll lose some sheep," he said, "we can't help it. But they ain't in too bad a place, if they'd settle down. I'll go back, soon as I can, and see if I can soothe 'em some."

They walked as fast as they could, taking thought of their footing, slower going back than they had been coming because now it was hard to see small objects that might trip them on the slick ground. They were nearing the dugout when they heard wolves howling.

"They're close," the man said.

The bleating of the sheep rose suddenly, then sank down, and changed to jerky, broken baas fading into the night.

"The fool things are a-running," he said. He put the lambs he carried on the ground. "Look after 'em, Dovie," he said. "I've got to go."

He ran to get his horse, which stood waiting to be put in out of the cold with the cow and the calf.

"Can't I come and help this time?" Mary Dove cried after him.

"No," he shouted, "you can do more good here."

Soon he rode off, old Shep running ahead of him, barking already, scolding the sheep.

While Mary Dove stood looking after them, longing to follow, she saw that the mist was changing to thick, swirling snow. And of course her father was right: there was much to do here, and with him she would only be in the way.

She hurried to carry the lambs in. Then she thought of her rabbit and, poking around behind the woodpile, found it and brought it in, too.

Cold had moved into the dugout now; the creatures there needed some heat. But she decided she had better rinse her bucket and cloth before the milk dried too hard on them, and she went to the spring. Ice was forming around the edge of the little shallow pool there. For some reason, finding that brought a sudden rush of fear. She did not know what she was afraid of, but now she was anxious to build a fire.

After she got the fire going, she sat on a bench in front of it and tried to think what she must do next. She remembered supper. Her father had gone off without eating, and she was sorry for that, but she guessed he was no hungrier than she was. He could eat whenever he came home.

That would surely be soon. It couldn't take him very long to get the sheep settled down in some good place. She wished he need not have gone, but never doubted he had to. They had to look after their creatures. She thought of them all, wishing each one could be kept from the cold. She dwelt upon the image of the little baby calf, was tempted to bring him in with the lambs, but remembered, with a tickle of comforting laughter inside her, how her father sometimes accused her of thinking she could mother some little animal better than its own mammy could. The cow herself was protected from the worst of the cold, and no doubt could take care of her calf.

Mary Dove thought about the chickens. Up in their roosting trees, how cold would they be? One time (longer ago than she could remember but her father told the tale) it had got so cold the chickens' feet froze off. She made up her mind to go and try to bring some of them in. There were a lot of them—she didn't know how many, and she could not save them all, but she saw she must do what she could.

In the end, she caught half a dozen of them, though they fluttered up high in the trees when she reached for them, and the rooster she managed to save scratched blood out of her arm.

As she carried the last chickens in, and the flock quieted down among the frozen branches, she could hear trees all around her cracking under the icy weight they bore.

In the dugout the lambs were asleep and the rabbit kept

still in a corner near the fire. The chickens, put down, scurried around frightened at first, but Mary Dove talked to them softly, telling them about the ice and the danger of their feet freezing off. At last they got calm, and Mary Dove, after piling more wood on the fire, seated herself before it to wait for her father. Now she felt warm and unafraid, and the firelight flickered on the red earth walls of the tiny life-filled room.

2

Far into the night Mary Dove kept awake listening for her father. She wrapped herself in a blanket and lay before the fire, studying the flames, adding wood when they died down. She could look a long time into a blazing fire and need nothing else, just as she could lie gazing up into shape-shifting clouds for the whole of a summer afternoon. At last she went to sleep, not meaning to; when she awoke it was cold, and without seeing any ray of light she knew it was morning. And her father had not come.

The animals were waking, feeling morning too. The chickens began scratching around on the earth floor, expecting breakfast. Mary Dove built up the fire with the last of the wood they had brought inside, and then strewed some crumbled cornbread which the chickens accepted unsurprised. She offered bread to the rabbit, too, and he nibbled at it.

She found a bottle that had been used before to feed motherless animals, and warmed some milk for the lambs. She poured some of the milk over cornbread for her own breakfast.

She was putting off going outside. When she realized what she was doing she told herself she was silly. There was no reason to dread going up into a snow-covered world. For in fact she loved snow. Snow was a rare thing in that country; some winters there never was enough to cover the ground, and in some none fell at all. But what joy when it came. Her father used to lead her out into a morning after snowfall, as though to view some present he had himself prepared for her. She almost thought he had: they had such fun then, when she was a little girl, jumping into snowbanks, rolling balls of snow down the hill.

Today the snow could bring no joy. This, of course, was the thing that held her back. Accepting that thought, she put on her heaviest wraps and went out to see what had happened in the night.

She had never seen so changed a world. Snow hid or changed the form of everything. No snow was falling now, but the sky was still heavy and gray. She had remembered snows sparkling, alive. This one seemed lightless and dead.

She stood under the brush arbor, where snow had drifted across the rock floor. She was not aware of cold, yet she shivered. "I am afraid of all that dead white snow," she said. She had a sense of it taking her father—not a mind-pictured scene, but a sense only—of losing him in all that lightless white. Almost, she felt herself lost in it.

The cow bawled. Mary Dove plunged out into the snow, which even where it had not drifted came up above her knees.

"I never saw such a snow," she said to herself. No wonder her father hadn't come. He had found a safe warm cave somewhere and had sense enough to stay in it till morning, but he would be coming soon.

Meanwhile, she had to see to things. The cow and calf were all right in their shed, and the calf had taken care of the milking. But the chickens, though protected from the worst of the snow, had frozen fast in their trees, their feet wrapped up with the limbs in layers of furry ice.

Mary Dove stared with horror a moment, then hurried back to the dugout. She carried in several armloads of wood. She could not think of anything to do now but keep a fire going. All through the morning she did nothing but pile on wood and watch flames leaping, while she listened for a step at the dugout door.

It never came. "He is not coming," she said to herself at last, but quickly added, "not today." Not today, because he is hurt. He slipped and fell—his horse fell with him—but he has found some shelter. He might not even be very far away. Or he might be miles away, in any direction.

It might be, he could hear her if she called. Or the dog might hear and come, might lead her to him. Several times that day she went out into the snow and called. She called and called to Shep, but got no answer. Snow began falling again; the earth was wrapped so thick in snow it seemed to deaden sound. Her shouts might bury themselves before they could reach her father's ears.

"But he will come," she said. "When the snow melts he'll come, or he'll send Shep."

When toward nightfall she went out one last time to scan the earth and sky, she saw, between them, across the west, a ribbon of pale gray light, prophecy of sunshine. The next morning she climbed out of the darkness into a world so dazzling she covered her eyes against it. This glittering, piercing whiteness was no more bearable than the lightless white of yesterday.

There was, however, when she looked again, the deep relieving blue of sky, which turned the sparkling day into something more strangely beautiful than she had ever dreamed of. She was not sorry to think, though, that the familiar warmth of the sun already lightly touching her would shortly wipe that scene away. Things would soon be right again.

Through the morning she took care of the animals and cleaned the dugout, which was beginning to stink from the ones she had kept there. She let the rabbit and chickens out, but kept the lambs; they had scarcely known any place but the warm dark insides of their mothers' bodies—she thought they would feel more at home in the dugout for a while.

When she took time to go back outdoors and stand looking out from the arbor, she saw the hard glitter was gone from the day. Though glare from the snow still made the sunshine unnaturally bright, there was a softening everywhere. The whole outdoors was dripping and trickling. The frozen chickens came loose from their trees and fell down into the snow, and their survivors came and pecked at them.

Mary Dove turned away from the sight but said to herself, "That's how chickens do, I reckon." She would take the dead ones off somewhere before they started to rot.

About noon, she knew her father was not coming. There was nothing now to keep him waiting in any hole or cave, unless he lay unable to move, in pain and hunger, waiting for her to find him. So she would go.

They lived at the head of a creek, and she decided to follow it as she believed the sheep might instinctively have done. She kept just above it, on high ground clear of the flooded creek bed, looking about her always for signs of the sheep or her father. Often she called the dog, but never did she hear or see a sign that she hoped for.

Away down the creek there was a rocky cave not big enough for much but an animal den, and that was her destination. She pictured her father there, having crawled into it after his horse fell injuring them both. Old Shep would be standing guard at the cave mouth, though no doubt, when he heard her calling, he would come running to greet her.

But she called and called, and he never came. She moved more slowly than she had expected, and when she reached the little cave the sun was low in the west. There was no one in the cave, no sign of human life though some animal had been using it. She sat down dejected on a ledge, as though this had been the only place in the world where her father could possibly be and now he was gone forever.

Tears flowed, the first since he had left her, and she gave herself up to sorrow while the shadows came up around her and over a hill somewhere wolves started howling.

At last she was roused by the sudden sense that another night of bitter cold was almost upon her. She rose hurriedly, half thinking that her father would be waiting at the dugout, worried because she was late, and then remembered no one waited for her there or ever would. That was wrong, though. The chickens and animals were there, wondering already why she did not come.

And then, as she walked homeward, putting her mind to the everyday jobs awaiting her, hope for her father came back. She had been silly. There were countless other places he might be–or he might be at the dugout when she got there.

He was not at the dugout. Day after day she looked for him, and came home with the slowly dying hope that she would find him waiting. At last she made up her mind to go across the hills and follow a creek she knew that ran northward. The sheep seldom grazed far down that creek, but occasionally she had gone to hunt the herd and found it in that direction.

It seemed to her that day that with her eyes shut she could almost believe the ice had never come and spring had been there always. A hundred small birds sang together, making a gurgling stream of sound, above which the meadowlark song repeatedly rose. In low places she could hear water moving, just deeper than birdsong, and everywhere was the smell of warm, wet earth.

There was another smell, too–one not unfamiliar to her, or offensive–a dead animal smell. As she moved near it, though, it began to seem overpowering–she had never known this odor so strong. And so she came upon a scene she was to see again, more than once, a pile of dead cows that, seeking shelter in a little hollow, had been caught and frozen there.

This was the way she would find the sheep. She had guessed why she never heard a sound of them, but before this had not really pictured how they might be if they had all run frightened together until they piled up somewhere and died, smothered or frozen.

The scene brought something else to mind, too. For several years she had occasionally seen bunches of cows on the range where, in the beginning, only the sheep had grazed. And once in a while she had seen a man on horseback riding near them.

The first time she saw him, she was with her father. He quickly caught her hand and pulled her back into the bushes.

"Don't never let him see you," he said hoarsely, whispering even though the man was too far away to have heard anything but the loudest shout. "Don't never let him come near you, and if any man ever comes to the dugout when I'm gone, stay out of sight and keep him from knowing you're there."

She was surprised at his harshness. She had grown up knowing she must never let anyone into the dugout or even let herself be seen, if she could help it, should a stranger come wandering by. The only people she could remember ever coming near their dugout, though, were some Indians in the very earliest years. She barely saw them as she peered from the dugout door, for her father kept her out of their sight. They didn't stay long–they were looking for good saddle horses, and her father had nothing that pleased them. He used to warn her about Indians, but it had been a long time since there was any danger from them. She did not know why there should ever be danger from anyone, but until they saw the man on horseback she had not thought to ask.

But then she sensed a sharp new urgency in her father's commandments and for the first time asked him why.

"If you ever need to know, you'll just know," he said. "You ain't big enough yet to understand it."

When she was very little he told her there was only one thing she ought to be afraid of–a rattlesnake; and if she was careful to watch and heed the snake's warning, then she need not be very much afraid of him.

"This is worse than rattlesnakes," her father said, "for a man may not give any warning."

So she had learned to be watchful, and when she saw the cows she remembered that the man might be somewhere near. Now she recalled that on the few occasions when she had seen him, he had been in the vicinity of that north-running creek and she thought, With Papa gone, I must be more careful even than I was before.

She was prepared, then, when she saw him. He appeared on a little rise, closer than he had ever been to her. She watched, hidden in thick brush. He stopped and she could see sweat running down from under his stained felt hat. He wiped his face with a black handkerchief, then swiftly rode away.

Mary Dove, her heart beating hard, stayed a long time in the bushes waiting to see if he would come that way again. At last she turned homeward. She could think of no reason why he would come back there that day, but having once seen him she felt too fearful to go on. Sometime she would come again, but she would remember to be watchful when she did.

When, after a few days, she had seen no living cattle anywhere, but had come upon more piles of rotting carcasses, she concluded that the cattle, as well as the man who took care of them, were gone. And so she went again to the north-running creek and made her way along it, on the high ground, to a place where the hillside broke off to become a high bluff.

Standing there looking down, she felt she had seen that sight before, so many times had she prefigured it. The great sodden mass of wool was no surprise. She did not notice the remains of the black horse until she went down into the creek bed, but she was not surprised at that either. Everything seemed falling out according to some design she recognized, and she expected that it would not take her very long to find her father's body. She was determined to find it, for her father had spoken to her of her mother's grave, left behind him many hundred miles, and she understood that people buried their loved ones in the earth.

But she looked a long time that day and returned again, and still again, and never found it, nor any sign of the old dog Shep.

"He is buried under the sheep, then," she said to herself at last. "I may find his bones some day."

3

Finding his bones to bury would be enough. Knowing what had happened was enough, really. It lifted a burden, and no greater sorrow came to her than she had known before.

In the last few days she had walked so far, ever straining her senses to the limit as she sought for any sign, that now, at the end, the thing she overwhelmingly realized was that she was tired. She knew a clear temptation to climb out on the hilltop, stretch out underneath the sky and sleep while the sun went down and the stars came out, and maybe through the rising and another setting of the sun, for she was so very tired. There were many reasons why she could not yield to that temptation–her animals at home the most urgent. And so she went back to them, slowly and dully, and did what they required before she descended into the dugout and gave herself up to sleep. When she awoke she had no sense of what time of day it was, though she could see through her open door that it was day. She lay a long time bringing together recollections of all that had happened, and then went up into the light.

It was nearly noon, bright noon. She stood under the brush arbor, getting used to the time and condition of the day, while her seven lambs crowded around her, their voices demanding, reproaching. The little bunch of hens came up onto the rock floor with impatient, questioning clucks–the rooster stood back pretending unconcern. The cow bawled, calling attention to herself and her calf. These, it came to Mary Dove, were all she had. She wondered about the rabbit–she had not thought about it for several days. Old Shep was gone, she knew now.

And her father. Was gone. Was nowhere. Was not ever coming back. (Or could he, some way?) No. Was not.

Now she stood at the door of her dugout, her creatures about her, and the rest of the world spread out endlessly, empty, all around. Suddenly she cast herself down on the cold stones and wept. Grief possessed her. She cried out, and moaned, and twisted her body scraping off skin on the rough stones.

At last she sat up and looked around her, and there they still were, her animals, standing curiously, not frightened off by her uncommon behavior.

"Poor things," she said.

She hugged a nuzzling lamb, and once again burst into tears, burying her face against its wool.

But this time she only wept, and the weeping was soon over. At last she stood up, wiped her face with the palm of her hand, and spoke to them. "Well, then, I'll take care of you," she said.

Through the days that followed, almost all she did was take care of them. Like a newly widowed mother, she made the lives that were left to her, depending on her, the only reason for living. She rejoiced when the rabbit came back, and even found roots and tender leaves of grass for it, bringing it into the dugout with her. It learned to hop up and down the steps, and came when she called "Rab."

If it had not been for the animals, she would have been consumed with the grief for her father, which seemed never-ending. Constantly she was reminded of the loss of his companionship. Even the silent times, when he would seem to be living unhappily alone in some place she never could go, seemed sweet to her, and she would have given anything just to see him sitting motionless beside some tree or rock, his eyes fixed on clouds or hazy hills.

Though once her greatest pleasure had been wandering down the creeks and over the hills, among birds and flowers, now she never went farther away from the dugout than the spring where she washed her face and rinsed her household utensils. When she was not busy at some necessary chore, she sat on a bench in the shade of the arbor and looked far away, seeing nothing.

As her father had done. She wished she had guessed, in his lifetime, what she believed she understood now. How lasting grief was, for the loss of a loved one.

Now this was a time of pure grief, for never once in those days did she think of anything his death might mean to her, except his absence from her.

4

One morning when she went to the cowshed the calf failed to rush into the pen, as he usually did, hurrying to his mother's teats the moment the gate was open. Instead, he sprang off playfully down the gentle, treeless slope that led to the little creek.

Impulsively, Mary Dove set down her bucket and ran after him, with the thought in her mind nevertheless that she might as well let him go, for if he didn't care whether he got his breakfast or not, then most likely he didn't need any.

For no reason, she ran, liking the feel of new soft grass under her feet (naturally, without conscious thought, she had left off her shoes one warm morning and had not worn them since). She lifted her skirt–already halfway up to her knees, she had grown so much since the last time her papa brought clothing from town–and ran freely after the calf, not even wanting to catch him. She lifted her chin, breathed deeply, and with her eyes on the soft blue, feather-clouded sky, tripped over a rock and fell.

Down among the grass and buttercups. She sprawled there, laughing, and the calf stopped and turned to look at her. He must have thought it strange to hear her laugh–she was surprised at the sound, herself.

There she was, down among the buttercups and laughing. How strange and new everything seemed–the green grass, the soft sky, the bright yellow flowers. She was laughing with joy at her realization that spring had come back and the earth had bloomed again.

How could she laugh?

With that question, the realization of her loss came over her, as it had done so many times, but gently, with no sharp stab of pain.

Then she got up and got her bucket and went in to milk, and the calf came back, wanting his breakfast more than he thought he had.

Later it seemed to her that on that day she woke up from a long, dream-troubled sleep. She did not know how many days of sunshine had passed, how many spring showers had fallen, since last she looked around with seeing eyes.

Perhaps some change had taken place at the bend in the creek where the sheep had died. She decided to go and see.

She started out slowly and sadly, not driven as she had been during the long searches after the storm, not blindly, as she had lately gone about her tasks, but calmly, knowing just where she was going, believing there was a reason.

In this way she was thinking when she heard little hoof-beats behind her and turned to see her lambs, the seven of them bunched together, following after her.

She laughed for the second time that day. "Oh you sillies," she cried, and ran back to the dugout, as they ran, too, all around her. She lured them into the dugout and left them there, shutting the door behind her. They were not ready yet to go so far, and she couldn't bear to lose them.

Now she started again, somewhat more cheerful than before, but sad and thoughtful, making her way over the hill. She had no doubt about what she would find, expected nothing more than before, but knew somehow that it was time to go and look again.

Not much had changed. She looked at what had been her father's horse–wondered briefly if she ought to try to save the saddle; but it would do her no more good than the rickety little old wagon by the cowshed. The mass that once had been a herd of sheep now made a small hill, diverting the creek around it. There was still no sign of man or dog.

All the creatures dead in the great storm were becoming earth, from which in some later spring–a year from now, or a hundred years–bright flowers would rise and bloom. That, it turned out, was the thing Mary Dove had come to see and ponder.

She guessed spring and earth went on forever, made out of lives God took to renew them, to renew them constantly as people kept putting fuel on a fire when they ran out of matches. Maybe God had no matches (so you might imagine, if you thought God was a man, as her father seemed to do)—maybe God had no matches, and if the fire ever went out spring and earth would end, the world would end. She guessed it never would end though, because life went on renewing life –going back to earth, coming out of earth, forever and ever. Because God was not a sheepherder in a dugout far from town, using up his matches. God was the fuel and the fire, and the fire builder too.

And now her father was with God, part of God, part of the fuel and the fire.

Or that thought came to her, as she stood above the rotting sheep. She used to ask her father about things that came to her this way–notions, funny notions, he had called them. But she learned he didn't know much about God, or didn't want to tell what he knew.

Once she had asked him about nearly this same thing–he had seemed unsure of the answer. It was long ago, or so she thought of it, but the range cows were there already, so it couldn't have been in the earliest days.

She walked with her father on a far hill, one bright morning at the very beginning of spring, before there was any tree in leaf or any flower blooming. She kept skipping ahead of him, eager as a calf or lamb, wanting to reach–whatever was there to be reached. And so she came well before him to a hillside just above a watering hole that the cows had been using in the fall and early winter. Her father said they had been moved to another range (otherwise he never would have brought her there), but they left many signs of themselves behind them.

It was these signs and what had happened to them that set her laughing. She plopped down on the dry grass among them and laughed so hard her father came running to her, astonished.

"Look!" she called to him. "Papa, look!" The words sputtered out between bursts of laughter.

He came and stood grinning down at her. She guessed, looking back now, he had been tickled more at her than at the funny thing she had found. She guessed it might not seem as funny to her now, but she was still a little girl and had never seen anything like it.

Neither had her father, though. "I ain't never seen that before," he said with his one-sided grin.

It was pats of cow dung, dropped all over the hillside, dried flat as hoecakes, and sprouting–every one of them–a clump of thick fresh yellow-green grass. There was nothing else growing green on that hill.

"Them cows eat that tall grass along the creek last fall, after it went to seed," her father said. "I reckon not having any rain so long dried these things out, and then the showers and warm weather come and set the grass a-growing."

"After the cows planted it," Mary Dove said, delighted.

"Right along with their own manure," her father said, and laughed with her.

Mary Dove took a stick and poked at one bunch of the grass. The roots had gone right down through the cow pat and into the ground. She could see that the pat was already breaking apart and would soon be part of the ground itself.

Her father hunkered near her and took a stick and poked too. They were in no hurry–or it might be that was just where they were going.

"I've seen stuff come up from cow droppings before," he

said, "but never did see it work just like this. Course a part of everything they eat goes back in the ground, and if there's seeds they'll come up."

Mary Dove's thoughts spread out from there. She thought of herself squatting in the bushes on the hillside behind the dugout. "What we eat goes in the ground, too," she said.

Her father grinned once more. "It shore does," he said.

She tried to think of everything that went back to earth. She remembered dead animals–sheep, rabbits, birds. What the buzzards didn't eat–what happened to it? Bones bleached a long time, through sun and rain, but even they must disappear at last, or else the land would be covered with them.

"Does everything finally get to be part of the ground?" she asked.

He poked among the dry grass, flipping out pebbles. "I reckon," he said.

"Animals," she said.

"Everything that lives," he said.

Her thoughts followed that idea awhile, and came to something startling. "Me?" she asked.

"Even you and me," he said.

It was the first time she quite knew they would die. She cried about it.

He moved and put his arms around her, tried clumsily to comfort her. "Everything that lives must die," he said, "but people's different."

Oh, she believed him. But– "How could that be?" she asked. "Don't we rot–like the birds and rabbits do?"

He stammered, not like himself–began to say something, then stopped and said something else. At last she seemed to have an answer, which was: yes we do, but somehow, even so, we go when we die to some place named Heaven, where we can be with God.

She had heard the name of God on his lips before (God help us, God knows), but it had not seemed to name a real or meaning thing, and she had never wondered.

"What is God?" she asked then.

"You ask that question funny, Mary Dove," he said.

"What had I ought to say?"

"Well–I reckon, *who*. They say God made man in his image."

God made everything, he went on to tell her, and God knows everything, and sees us all the time, whatever we do, and knows when we keep his laws or break them. "My mammy told me all that," he said, "a long time ago."

"If God is a man why can't we see him?"

"Well, he's not a man exactly–and you just can't see God."

"How do you know God is there?"

He shook his head. "You ask too many questions, Dovie," he said gently, then seemed to think of something: "They say you can feel his presence. Some folks can anyway, and they tell about it, and that's how come people knows as much as they do."

She thought about all he said. "I don't think God could be a man though," she said at last.

"Well, you may be right, Dovie," he said. "I never did know much about God."

Afterwards, she began to believe that she knew what it was. What God was. Or anyway (if this was how you said it) knew what his presence felt like. No wonder her father couldn't explain, because God must be so far from being like people that the kind of talk people used couldn't say anywhere near what God was.

She began to believe that a strange and powerful feeling she experienced sometimes was the effect upon her of God's fleeting presence. She never tried to describe this feeling to her father, partly because she knew no words that could even suggest it and partly because she suspected he would rather not know. But she cherished this new understanding, and when there came to her (as always, from time to time, there had come) an emptiness or a sadness or even a wild joy that she could not explain to her father, she would go and secretly seek the presence, finding in it consolation or fulfillment or relief.

Now for the first time since her father left her, she remembered this help she might get: Was something like this what he meant when he used to mutter "God help us"?

She determined to go now and call to her this feeling–this help. Though it might come anywhere, unsought, at the sight of a flower or the sound of some bird, she had learned she could find it most surely and feel it most strongly in certain places that since early childhood she had especially loved.

One of them was the large clear pool a little below the spring they used, around a bend in the creek from it and out of sight of the dugout. There were other places, good at certain times: a treeless hilltop at sunset in winter, a shady hollow in summer with daisies among the grass, sometimes just bare flat rocks along the creek where the feeling moved through her as she baked like a lizard in the sun.

But most kinds of times she liked the deep pool best. Many years ago, her father had taught her to bathe in it. She had learned to swim naturally and loved to move around under the water, among the little yellow perch that lived there.

One long-ago time at the pool had stayed alive as the present moment in her memory. It was a warm noonday in fall. She knew the water would be cold, but she ran down the sloping rock shore into the water and plunged into the deepest part, down to the bottom of the pool. The cold hit her so hard that for a moment she seemed to see nothing, feel nothing; then, getting used to it, she stayed swimming down in the green water until she had to come up for breath.

When she came up and onto the rocks that surrounded the pool, she looked up through cottonwood trees at a sky that was so strong and pure a blue that its very blueness seemed to beat against her. She lay back on smooth warm sandstone and looked up, her eyes drawn to the sky–looked up through cottonwoods, and the leaves on the trees were yellow as yellowest butter, in summertime when grass grows thick and green. The force of that yellow and blue almost scared her, and yet she could not turn her eyes away but kept looking until she began to feel somehow drawn out of herself, no way she could explain or even start to understand, but being pulled, and yearning painfully to go, though bound there, on her rock.

Slowly, by some magic, as she lay still and waiting, the yearning passed. She could not have said what she longed for, or when–if at all–she received it; yet at the end she was calm, content, and utterly at peace with herself and the world around her.

Only afterwards did she guess at the word for what happened to her then, and begin to invite it.

The pool was always a calm and separate place, cut off by a steep bluff on one side, hidden by a thick growth of trees on the other. Above it one bank of the creek sloped gently, but Mary Dove, coming from the dugout, followed a narrow trail along the steep side of the creek. She had sometimes come upon wild animals drinking at the pool, but the irregular rock shore kept herds of sheep or cattle away, so that the spot was always quiet and the water undisturbed.

Now the thick willows, once blackened by the freeze, had greened again, and cottonwood leaves whispered in a light south wind. A dove, who always lived in a dead hackberry tree that stood among the cottonwoods, cooed at her unfrightened; little green frogs splashed into the water, escaping, not knowing yet who she was.

She stood on the broad, smooth rock that sloped into the water, listening, waiting.

Oh, she loved this place the best. Only in the last two or three years, she had stopped coming much, except to take a bath. That was because of a change in the way her papa taught her to do.

When she was getting ready for bed one night he said to her, "Mary Dove, I reckon you had better quit undressing in front of me now."

"Why, Papa?"

"You're getting too big. Men and women just ain't supposed to see each other naked, and you're getting to be a woman now."

"But I'm still Mary Dove, just the same."

"No, there's a difference now. Your mother would tell you, if she was here, explain it better than I can, but all you need to know is it's a law of God."

It seemed a funny law to her, but she didn't ask him questions about God any more. She believed, anyway, that he knew God's laws—there were people somewhere that knew all about God, and he had learned from them.

It was a law of God that children must do what their fathers told them to, and so she did. But she had to change her ways. She had always liked to stand at the poolside with her body bare, feeling the sun and wind full on it, or to lie awhile on the warm rocks when she came out of the pool. But one day as she stood so, rapt and still in the sunshine, her father came along.

"Now you mustn't stand out like this," he said to her. "Take your bath, and when it's done with get back in the trees and get dressed."

But today there was no one to see what more she did than take a bath. She stood on the flat smooth rock and lifted her dress over her head. She had to struggle with it—it was too tight, and she had to free herself from it.

The south wind blew softly. She liked its gentle touch, but she did not mind a sharper wind, either. She stood feeling the wind and listening to the leaves, while she unbraided her long dark hair. She had always worn it in two thick plaits, as her father had taught her to do. "It's so fly-away," he said, "that if you don't hold it down some way it'll be catching on bushes and getting pulled out, like the sheep's wool does."

He was right. It was better, going through her ordinary days, to have it pulled out of her face, bound out of the way of things. But she wanted it free now, with the wind blowing through it.

She was nearly ready. Waiting, listening, she began to sing in a voice that held some hint of the sound of leaf whispers. She often sang–her father said she had a sweet voice like her mother's. He had taught her all the songs he knew, but they were songs to be sung to him as she played her mother's old guitar.

For these times, she made up little songs. Really, she didn't call them songs. She had made up a few songs and sung them to amuse her father–songs more like the ones he knew, with words that rhymed and verses that told tales. Now she simply opened her mouth and sang as birds do. She never tried to remember the words or tunes, but she knew the same ones often came back to her, until at last she had special things to sing, for special times and places, and yet made them over, new, each time she sang, changing some of the words, putting in new ones, not singing quite the same notes every time.

"Whisper whisper"
(she sang)
"Whisper leaves, tell me
Whisper me God,
Whisper me what is in you, that is God

"While wind blows God
South wind brings God,
Cottonwood leaves, narrow willow leaves,
All green and greeny yellow leaves
show me God
and little green frogs sing God
and in the water, splashing in the green water,
find God,
Washing, water washing,
washing everything not God out of me

"And I come out new,
like the little frog
and the unspeckled leaf,
Clean and new,
Drying in the south wind."

She plunged into the pool. It came over her. What she yearned for was coming over her. When it came, all grief, all uncertainty, even all concern with what belonged to her to do, the care of her creatures, would be gone for a while.

When it was over she stayed motionless on the flat rock, keeping all she could inside her for a long time. Frogs came out of the pool and sat poised on the edge near her. A tiny brown bird appeared on a willow twig and sang a song like thin ice falling down from high branches. A dove came and perched so near she could have touched it, then flew to its hackberry limb and sadly called to her.

"Was I named for the dove, or was it named for me?" she asked her father once. She had forgotten his answer—for a long time, she thought they were sisters, not understanding then what a sister was, and still in fancy kept that old belief.

At last, the sun and wind having dried her, she went and got a comb that she kept in the crotch of a tree and then sat again by the water's edge and spent a long time combing her thick tangled hair.

The sun was low in the west before she braided her hair and pulled her hot, confining dress down over her body. It was time to go back to the dugout where her animals waited for her.

She went back as she always had done, reluctantly, and yet with one new thought: one guess. What had come to her that day was that nothing ended because everything belonged to God. Flesh rotted and turned to earth or was eaten and taken straight back into life again. This she had long known, and seen again that day. But this was not all. With people—with her father, though he rotted like the sheep—there was something more, as he had once told her without knowing how that could be. The part of a person that reached out toward God (unseen, as God was) did reach God at last and stayed there not for little bits of time (as she had done) but always, never ending, a new being made of nothing but clear joy.

5

The next morning as Mary Dove went to milk, she looked around her. As yesterday her eyes had been opened to flowers blooming and her ears to birdsong, today the immediate scene around her dwelling place came freshly into her view, as though it had been shut off a long time by a curtain of fog.

"The corn!" she exclaimed.

She never had planted the corn. There was the square of broken ground, on a level place down toward the spring. Her father had gone over the ground with his little walking plow, and the day the ice came they had been breaking up clods with shovel and hoe, getting ready to plant the corn.

Well, she would plant it. There would be no early roasting ears, as they had planned, but she could raise a crop that would have time to ripen for winter use. She found bean and squash seed, stored from last year, to plant spaced out among the corn, as they were accustomed to do.

At the end of a long hot day's work she went and washed herself at the spring, then brought her bowl of cold cornbread and milk out under the brush arbor where she could feel the cool air on her face and watch the evening light change and darken into night. In those days she usually built a fire only in the early morning and cooked what she would need for the day. Some days she never built a fire at all, if she had enough bread already cooked.

The chickens had gone to roost, and the lambs were bunched up by the dugout for the night. She could see the cow and calf from where she sat, but she supposed Rab the cottontail had gone hopping off into the brush. She let him go free, against her real wishes, for she knew there might be a morning when he would not be waiting for her by the dugout door. It was better to leave everything to its own nature, though: Rab might become a coyote's meal, but as a little girl she had learned that all her love and care couldn't change a wild animal's ways.

What she had to do, she thought, was look after the animals that depended on her because they had always been taken care of and did not know nature's ways. And herself. Of course, she had to take care of herself now.

She looked down at her smooth planted patch and felt good about it. There was the promise of plenty to eat, for all of them. Fresh vegetables for the summer, dried ones for winter, and corn that (besides what she cracked for chicken feed) would make her bread and mush for many months.

So she mused, letting her thoughts slip slowly by, watching the last sunset color fade from the drifting fragments of cloud.

Corn ground into meal–that was the thing they had always depended on the most. Her father took the shelled corn to town every fall and had it ground into meal that would do them until fall came around again.

Her father took the corn to town.

But he would never go to town again.

She had learned to believe that his earthly love for her was ended, his daily presence gone from her forever. She had relinquished him to God, and in her own renewed experience of God thought she had found the way to do without her father. She had remembered, even, that she would have to provide for her physical needs; but the full realization of all that necessity would mean came to her now for the first time.

Her father had gone to town–twice a year, in spring and fall. He left before daylight one morning and came home the next day, late at night. He had never taken her with him, and although she had an idea that town was somewhere south of them, a long day's journey, she could not begin to imagine how she would ever find the way to get there, or what she would do if she did.

She had a dim and clouded picture in her mind of what town must be like, for before they came to this hillside they had lived in one. But that had been so long ago that she could not remember their leaving, or the journey, or the building of the dugout. Sometimes she thought she could remember houses, built all on top of the ground, out of boards like the ones her father had brought home to make a tight door for the dugout—houses all close together in a row like cornstalks. But other times she thought this might be just a picture she made up out of little bits of things her father said.

He never did say very much. To her questions, he only answered that town was no place to go unless you had to, and no place to think about as long as you had the good luck to live far away from it.

It seemed to her that when she could first remember his going, he used to shut her in the dugout. But he must not have liked to do that, for through all the time she could clearly remember he had left her free to go and come as she pleased.

But he never left without telling her, always the same thing over again, the way she must do in his absence.

"Now don't get very far away from the dugout. Keep a watch-out all the time for anybody that might come prowling 'round here, and if you ever see a soul keep out of sight. Get in the dugout if you can, and bolt the door. Don't never open that door to nobody. I don't care who it is, or what they tell you—just don't never let nobody come into this dugout."

Last year he had said to her, "I hate to leave you, Dovie. I worry more than ever now, you've got to be such a big girl."

And she, for the first time wondering, had said, "Why don't you take me with you, Papa, if it worries you to leave me by myself?"

A strange thing happened then. It was not an unheard of thing—it was something that had happened once in a while in her life, but so seldom that it came always with a frightening shock, as if he had struck her a blow (a rarer thing still).

"You ask that!" he shouted. "I've told you a hundred times, and you ask it. I've told you how bad town is, I've told you and told you, and you ask it."

He began to pace around the dark little room where they lived.

"Are you starting to think I'm just a old man that don't have good sense? I tell you, Mary Dove, you had just better listen to me, and keep listening. You try to put yourself above me, you'll be sorry, I can tell you that!"

His voice had risen to a roar, filling the dugout. "I've brought you here, and took care of you, and you turn on me now!"

She tried to protest, explain, but he never paused to hear her. He picked up a crockery pitcher that had held their supper milk, lifted it high and hurled it to the floor. It broke to pieces.

"You'd be just like that pitcher if you ever went to town. I'd rather leave you here a hundred years than take you. I'd just as lief see you in hell."

The last words were almost indistinguishable. He had almost lost control of his tongue, as of his actions. He picked up a bowl, seemed about to hurl it like the pitcher to the floor, then set it down and without another word or look to Mary Dove stumbled up the steps and out into the night.

He came back next morning, gentle and sorry. He hugged her against him and kissed her tenderly, begging forgiveness. "It's a way I am," he said. "I wish to God I could help it, but I can't. There's things that come back to me, Mary Dove, things that maybe you ought to know but I can't never tell you. If you love me you never will ask."

"I never will, Papa," she said.

"I can see why it come to you to ask that question," he went on. "If you wasn't such a good daughter to me you'd have doubted me long before. I never aimed to keep you out here away from everybody forever. But somehow I can't never think of any other way."

"I didn't mean nothing, Papa," she explained. "I didn't doubt you, I only wondered. I don't never want to live no other way but here with you."

"But some day I won't be here no more. People gets old, and they die."

"But that'll be a long time, Papa."

"Yes, a long time," he said. "I'll figure out a way."

But it hadn't been so long and Mary Dove guessed he never had thought of any way. She wondered and wondered what he might have thought of, what he ever could have done that would have changed her life. She could not imagine anything but living in the dugout, and that night she began to think—for the first time to clearly think—of how that life would have to be.

For she could not go to town. Her father had gone and brought back many things. Things to eat: sugar and salt, a little wheat flour, dried fruit, such simple ordinary things. She was astonished to discover there would come a time when she would have to do without them. Clothes: shoes and stockings, overalls for him, a dress for her and some years a coat. Underwear.

And he had taken the corn to the mill.

There was a shallow round hole in a rock by the creek. Her father said he thought it was where Indians used to grind corn, when they camped there long ago. This came to her, and she knew she could grind corn. Only a little at a time, but she would not need much. She could have meal. Other things she would have to learn to do without. She could use them sparingly, and they would last a long time—the sugar and salt and soda would. At last she would simply have to find something else to use. She remembered her father had told her about a salty place over north somewhere, that animals used; maybe she could find her way there and get something that would do for salt. Her father had found bee trees sometimes—she might get wild honey for sweetening.

She wouldn't starve as long as she could grow a garden, keep her chickens and a cow. She was lucky she had a bull calf. Her father had let the cow mate with range cattle, the last year or two, but if they were gone she could wait for the calf to grow. She wished she had a way to spin and weave the sheep's wool into cloth, as her father had told her women used to do. Since she had no way to sell the wool, they wouldn't do her much good otherwise. Her father said some people would eat sheep, but he never wanted to; and now Mary Dove thought she would rather starve than eat the flesh of any of her lambs.

She had dresses, but she had grown so much that her father had meant to get her some new ones this year. There was still a way, though, that she might get some clothes–a way she had always known about but seldom remembered. There was a trunk of her mother's things. "You can have 'em some day," her father had said. Except for the guitar, that was all there was of her mother. Her father had locked the trunk many years ago, before he brought Mary Dove into the wilderness, and never wanted to look into it. He said there was nothing in it but clothes, which would be no use to them until Mary Dove was grown. Then he would give her the key and they would be hers. She didn't know whether she was big enough to wear them yet–didn't know, really, whether or not she might be grown–but she guessed clothes that were too big would be better than those that she couldn't get into. She had a needle and thread and could hem them up, if necessary. She remembered she would have to be saving with thread, though.

Sitting while night came, she thought about all these things. She decided that tomorrow, by daylight, she would look for the key to the trunk.

She did not find it. She searched through everything in the dugout, but it was not there. She went to the trunk itself. They had always kept their bedding piled on top of it–blankets, an old pieced quilt, some coarse cotton sheets and pillow cases. She took all that off and examined the trunk. It was securely locked, as she had thought, and she knew that somewhere her father had had a key. She decided she would look longer. Somewhere, somehow, there must be a place she had overlooked–unless, of course, her father had kept it always with him, in the little pocket book he carried. But she would wait. There would be some way she could break the lock, but she didn't like to think of damaging the trunk. She would wait awhile, and see.

Meanwhile she put away her outgrown dresses and began wearing nothing but a loose white short-sleeved shift. It would be enough, till winter came, and by then she might have found the key.

6

Till winter came–and winter was far away–her life would be easy and free as the summertime of a songbird. Or would have been, she thought, except for one thing. Her silly lambs. She felt assured that her other creatures would be safe as long as the weather was good, but she could never tell what predicament the lambs would get into.

They followed her everywhere. Most of the time she didn't care if they did, and she liked their company, but one moonlight night a thing happened that made her decide she must take some step to protect them.

She had moved her straw mattress out onto the rock floor beneath the brush arbor, as she and her father had always been accustomed to do in the summertime, and she had taken to lying on it for a nap in the heat of the day, when even the birds and animals were still and the rasping of dry-weather bugs in the trees went on the same so long it became like part of the silence.

Then, after her nap, she would feel in the cool of the evening as if she never wanted to go to sleep again, especially on nights so warm and bright that the birds would start singing at twilight and never hush till dawn.

On nights like that, she used to take her mother's guitar and play and sing for her father. He knew nothing at all of how to get music from its strings, but he said he had saved it and brought it west because he hoped Mary Dove could play for him some day. He told her he had seen people hold down the strings with fingers of one hand while they picked and strummed with the thumb and fingers of the other. From that, she figured out a way to play. He liked it. He said it didn't sound exactly like the way he had ever heard anybody else play the guitar, but it had a kind of a sweet and lonesome sound about it that appealed to him.

Some of the songs he taught her were quick little funny songs, and sometimes she would play and sing one of them while he would dance a jig. His favorite went like this:

Raccoon's got a bushy tail,
Possum's tail is bare–
Rabbit ain't got no tail a-tall,
Just a little bunch of hair.

They used to laugh a long time together at the sound of that song and the figure he made jigging to it.

"Everybody knows that's the truth, Papa," she remembered saying one time, "so why did they make up a song about it?"

"I never could figure out the why of any song," he said. "I reckon folks just makes 'em up to suit the way they happen to feel, different times."

Most of the songs he knew were about lovers, parted by distance or death. He liked "Listen to the Mocking Bird" and "Barb'ry Ellen." Her own favorite was "Mohee," because in the end the lover was thinking about going back to his beloved, but she wished there had been one more verse telling how they really got together again. That was such a sad-sounding song, she could never be sure.

"Is it always sad to have a sweetheart?" she asked her father a long time ago.

"Nearly always," he said. "Sweet and sad, and you wouldn't want to do without the sadness if you had to miss the sweetness too."

"Will I ever have one, Papa?"

"I don't know," he said.

He got up and walked away from her, leaving her singing with her guitar, and didn't come home until late in the night.

The next day he said to her, "Maybe you will have a sweetheart some day, Dovie. Maybe I'll find you one sometime, and bring him home to you."

She used to imagine that someday he'd bring her a sweetheart from town, instead of sugar candy or a ribbon for her hair. She guessed she had never quite given up that dream. Till now.

She was restless. She stopped singing and began to play slowly, absently, not thinking any tune. The plucked strings sent sad echoing sounds into the night.

The sounds seemed to travel on, far over the hills, and turn and come back to her. But it was not guitar notes coming to her through the night—she stopped playing to listen. What she heard was coyotes, barking and howling, mingling their voices together, making music she had often heard before. Oh she had heard it before, but never had it called her so relentlessly as now. She put down her guitar and got up, walking as it seemed aimlessly, listening, wondering, unwittingly moving in the direction from which the call came. She did not know how far she had gone when she realized she was moving toward the source of that wild music. And wasn't that, she asked herself, a crazy thing to do? But she went on, ran lightly on.

She came to where a little bare hill strewn with smooth, moonshiny pebbles rose before her, and she knew that when she climbed it she would see what she had come to see. She paused. Something strong as fear gripped her. It was as though she would now come face to face with what had always been calling, calling, when she did not know how to go.

She went on to the crest of the hill, and it was there. Below her, on a flattened shoulder of that same hill, she saw the sight.

A ring of coyotes, close together, their heads lifted to the moon.

The music rose around her. The circle of coyotes, like some great planned design, seemed to invite her to join it. She stood poised on the hilltop, tempted, half believing she would go.

Some little noise behind her–rolling pebbles–made her turn around, and there–moving lightly toward her, coming up the hill–were her seven silly lambs, washed white as snow by the moonlight.

She ran down to meet them, whispering, "Come back, come back. I have led you to your oldest enemy."

But when they saw her coming they turned around and started homeward, and she was following them.

They went along silently together, the lambs falling into place all around her; she was still so nearly consumed by the sight she had seen that she did not think of scolding them.

But the next day she did. She told them how silly they were, and what kind of trouble they were going to get into, wandering around that way. Mostly she was telling herself, for she knew the lambs wouldn't listen.

She could not allow them to go rambling around like that, she said to herself. And yet how could she stop them? Usually, she thought, they would not leave their place by the dugout at night, and yet she couldn't tell what they might take it into their heads to do on some night of bright moonshine. She did not think they would ever go far away, unless they were following her, but still it worried her to have them unprotected. She made up her mind that she would have a pen and shelter for them, like the one her father had built for the larger animals. They had never had a place to keep the sheep; there had always been so many of them it would have been hard to fix a place big enough. But she could surely build a pen and shelter big enough for seven lambs.

She decided to let them keep their place near the dugout, where they had grown accustomed to spending the nights. For days she worked, cutting willow stakes for the pen, driving them far into softened earth, as she had seen her father do. Then for the shelter, instead of using brush from the thorny bushes nearby, she went over the hill north, to where scattered cedars grew, and cut branches from them, as her father had done for their brush arbor. This was more troublesome, and took longer, but she liked the smell of drying cedar and the look of it on her arbor, and she wanted the best for her lambs. As she said to herself, she had plenty of time. Before she finished, she might renew her own roof with fresh cedar.

Thus she filled her days—besides caring for her animals and her garden, fishing sometimes in her pool, and now and then wandering along the creeks and across the hills, as she had always done, finding birds' nests, flowers, and smooth soft-colored stones, for no other reason than the pleasure these things gave her.

Then one morning, though the sun shone warm, a light little wind blew out of the north and the sky, though cloudless, held something that made it less blue.

And winter was no longer far away.

7

Well then. She, like the animals, had to get ready for winter. She could tell the days were shorter, and she had a sudden sense of urgency, as though—like the ants hurrying down their little trails with heavy loads of seed—she must fill her daylight hours with bustling tasks.

Really, there was not so much need to hurry. What she wanted was to say to winter that it would not catch her unawares, she would be ready. There was plenty of time to gather the corn and shell it, pick the dried beans from their vines, find a dozen jobs to do that might have waited, only she was seized with the need to prepare.

She dragged in dead wood from creeks and hillsides, piling it near the dugout against the threat of wet and cold.

(She had decided to gather this wood that had broken from trees under the weight of ice and snow in the spring. She would spare herself some chopping, and save living trees as well.)

There was plenty of time, she knew, but as she ranged forth hunting wood she saw signs of the changing of seasons. Doves had stopped nesting, and were coming together to sit and wait (for what, she had asked them before and never learned) on high tree limbs. Quails were bunching; would burst up from the ground in front of her, as frightening (for an instant) as the spring of some hunting animal. She said to herself that she would catch some of them later in her father's bird trap, for the roosters she still had from among the hens' summer chickens would not make her many more meals. Her life was like the other lives around her, taking what it needed to sustain itself: she loved all the birds, but life was her strongest instinct.

Sensing this, she could take the loss of Rab without much mourning. One day, stroking him, she thought how his thickening fur was another sign of the season of the year. The next morning when she came out of the dugout he was not in his accustomed place. Though she called and searched for him, she never expected to see him again, and she did not. It was one of those singing moonlit coyotes that had eaten Rab. So she believed, and without rancor. She guessed the farther ranging of the coyotes was another sign that fall was near.

She was glad she had built the pen for the lambs. The calf, she thought, was so big now that a coyote wouldn't bother him, and her chickens roosting in their trees were safe out of a coyote's reach.

A few days later she saw a hawk carry off one of her young pullets. She ran shouting at him, throwing sticks, but he paid her no mind. She spent a time hating the hawk, letting anger override concern for her chickens (for herself, really, threatened with loss of meat and eggs and their chatty companionship). She kept shouting at him long after he had disappeared with the pullet.

But then, of course, afterwards she knew there was no use hating the hawk. It was a hawk's way, killing chickens. Likewise it was the way of owls, coyotes, skunks, possums, ground squirrels, bobcats, snakes, coons, foxes—the threat of them all came suddenly down, a heavy weight upon her; and she knew how silly it was to think the chickens were safe in the trees, for of course they never were safe, day or night—their chickens never had been.

What she had forgotten was the difference it made, having only a handful. Her father had always tried to keep chickens enough that he could, as he said, afford to lose a few. And he had fought constantly—with steel trap and gun—against all things that preyed on sheep or chickens.

Mary Dove could not fight his kind of battle, but she would have to save the chickens if she could. Could she have lost some already, without having missed them? This question came to her, and she knew she could have, for they scattered during the day and it had not occurred to her lately to count them. When they went to roost that night, she searched them out among the branches and, counting again and again as they shifted their positions, she could find no more than fourteen. She had had a dozen hens, and almost as many roosters, counting the ones that survived the freeze and the young ones hatched during the summer.

Oh how foolish she had been, when she ought to have been so careful. All the next day she kept track of the chickens, but at night when she counted them again one more was gone. She was almost sure of that: there was one hen less, and she needed to be especially careful about the hens.

Of course she might have counted wrong, but she didn't think she had. No chickens had been caught during the day; therefore something must be getting after them at night. She made up her mind that she would stay awake and find out what it was–she was still sleeping underneath the brush arbor, and could move her bed to where she could see the chicken trees.

When she found out what it was getting the chickens she would do something against it. She didn't know what she would do.

She hated and feared the steel traps her father used, had never even tried to set one. He said they were too strong for her anyway, she might hurt herself if she tried. She remembered, too, that he had not always had much luck setting traps near the dugout for any particular prowling animal. Most of his successful trapping was done farther away from home, for skins he could sell when he went to town.

Mary Dove had always turned away from the look in the eyes of those creatures caught by the biting steel. Nor could she bear the sight of them dead and denuded, or of their skins stretched to dry.

"Let me show you how, you can help me," her father said one time–she was just a little girl. He was skinning a coon: she looked and, feeling herself torn like it, ran off screaming.

He let her go without protest, but later said to her, "You're sure a funny youngun, Mary Dove."

"I just couldn't," she said.

He seemed to know all she meant by that and said, "It's all right. But it's funny, too–you can wring the head off of a chicken and skin it or pick the feathers off and never blink a eye. I reckon I've seen you eat a skint rabbit all right, too."

"I guess it's silly, Papa," was all she could think how to say. She liked to work with him, go with him to see to the sheep, help with any job, be by his side. And she could kill and dress things–chickens, wild birds, even rabbits–that they needed for food; but seeing the bare bloody bodies cast away, feeling (almost) the nails driven through stretched skin were more than she could bear.

She did not even try to explain all this to her father, but he said to her, "I get money for the skins, you know, and buy things we need pretty bad."

Yes, she was silly. She was silly, but she couldn't help it.

She was the same way about the gun. Her father had always kept a rifle: when he was gone it was with him and when he was at home it stood loaded by the dugout door. One time, after Mary Dove was getting to be a big girl, he brought a second rifle home from town. He said she had to learn how to use it. He said he would feel a lot better about going off and leaving her if she had a gun she could shoot.

She hated the gun, was afraid of it. She never quite believed it wouldn't go off and kill of its own accord, never trusted herself to control it. But she learned to load it and shoot, shuddering every time she pulled the trigger and heard the shell explode. At last she even learned to hit, most of the time, the trees that he told her to shoot at for practice.

Then one day he said to her, "See if you can hit that cottontail yonder."

She lifted the gun, then put it down again.

"I can't," she said.

"You ain't tried yet," he said.

"I just can't shoot a rabbit."

He walked away without saying anything. For a good while he never asked her to shoot, or even mentioned the gun to her.

Then one day he came and called her from her work down in the dugout.

"Get your gun and come with me," he said. "I want to show you something."

He led her to where a yellow-backed rattlesnake, as big around as her upper arm, lay coiled among some grass near the cowpen. He went so close that the snake reared its head and shook its heavy-rattlered tail in dreadful warning.

"Can you shoot a snake?" he asked her.

She half whispered, "I can try."

"Aim at its head," he said.

She killed the snake. She shot three times, at close range, and never did hit it in the head, but she killed it.

"Well, I reckon you won't be no marksman," he said, "but I see you can shoot if you need to."

She felt shaken, but she said, "I guess so, Papa."

"Now tell me," he said to her then, "do you think you could shoot at a man?"

"You mean could I kill somebody?"

He gave her a little one-sided smile. "Well," he said, "I reckon it would be a accident if you done that."

"Would I have to try?" she asked, not quite understanding him.

Then there was no smile on his face or in his eyes. "You might, Mary Dove," he said. "Now remember this. If ever I'm gone–gone to town, it might be, or just away somewhere out of calling distance–and you see any stranger a-coming, you get in the dugout fast, and you bolt the door. But if some way you can't get it shut against him, or he manages to break it down, you have the gun ready. And if he takes one step towards you, you shoot. Don't just threaten him, and wait to see what he'll do. Shoot!"

She could not answer him.

"It would be just like shooting that snake," he said.

In the end he made her promise, and if the thing that he feared ever happened, she believed she could do what he said.

But since the snake, she had never shot anything. She hated guns, and she hated steel traps. She had believed–or would have, if she had thought about it–that she could take what little she needed to eat, and protect the creatures that depended on her, without the use of either one.

Now she couldn't tell. If there were any way to use the gun or traps against this new threat–would she? She didn't know. She counted her chickens and tried to watch for the varmint that hunted them–but she didn't know.

The chickens were being taken slowly from her. Not every day would she find one missing, but now and then, and perhaps only when she had begun to hope the danger was past, she counted one less at roosting time. Twice she found little bunches of feathers among some bushes near the creek.

One night she found there were left to her only four hens and one rooster, and she climbed after them, caught them, and put them squawking into the dugout. They would have to learn to sleep there, she told them, until she found some better way to save them.

She still slept outside, as she meant to do till cold drove her (like the animals) back into her den, but this night she no longer had any idea of staying awake to watch for the chicken killer. If he came, he would be disappointed. In her relief and exhaustion she fell asleep as soon as she lay down. Then in the dark of the night there ripped into her deep sleep a chilling, piercing scream like the cry of some creature in terrible pain.

She sat up rigid on her narrow bed, gripping a blanket, waiting. And yet she needed no repetition of that sound. She knew what it was. She heard her father's voice cry hoarsely "Panther!" so strong did past fears come to her now.

A late moon had risen, not giving much light. For a little while she sat motionless, trying to peer into the shadows, though not expecting to see anything. That piercing cry had seemed far down the creek. She knew sound at night could fool you, but she didn't think there was a panther anywhere near the dugout. Not now. Nevertheless she wrapped her blankets around her and went to spend the rest of the night with the chickens on the dugout floor.

The panther was a secret kind of creature. Even her father could tell little of that animal, except tales he had heard far away from there when he was a boy. He dreaded it more than any other animal that preyed on his herd, though he lost more sheep to coyotes. Years sometimes went by without sign of the panther, and then one night would come the fearful scream. Even then they might hear no more of the beast, might see no signs of it. Or it might kill several sheep in one night and never give away its presence by a sound. Her father had glimpsed it dimly by night, but never close enough to get a shot at it, or even say exactly what it looked like.

They had always spoken of the menacing beast as the panther, as if there were only one, for all time. It was like a killer that roamed the whole world, like something beyond natural law, for they could never learn its habits. They never knew when it might come, how long it might stay, or what damage it would do. That night she wasn't even thinking of what it might do. Fear of the panther was deeper down than thought.

8

Next morning when she went to the spring to wash her face the bloody remains of her calf lay at the edge of the little pool. She stared, stunned, a moment, and then with an anguished cry ran to her lambs. All seven were there in their pen, huddled together. They came close to her, butting against the fence, telling her their fear in short nervous *baas*. She went in to them, let them all come knocking against her.

"I won't let him get you," she told them. "You'll be safe in your pen, it's all right."

Yet she wondered if she told them the truth. They were so strong now, and always pushing so. Was the fence she had made strong enough to hold them? Couldn't the panther, anyway, come down the hill onto the roof of the arbor and spring right into the midst of them?

She remembered her father had told how a panther might attack a herd in the night and kill a dozen or more sheep just for the fun of the killing. Oh, she hadn't remembered the panther when she built that pen. She had forgotten that deadly enemy.

She measured with her eye and tried to guess the distance a panther could jump. She did not know, really, whether he could reach the lambs, but something as clear to her senses as the rattle of a snake repeated "Danger."

"I won't betray you, I won't betray you," she said to them. She was not sure what betray meant, she remembered it from a song; she meant she would not fail them, she would save them from the panther, or die trying. Yes, that was what she meant.

She let them out. "He won't hurt you now," she said to them. "He don't feel like nothing but sleeping today–he's full of tender calf."

It was only then–saying that–that her mind came free enough from the fear of what might happen to the lambs to take in what had happened to the calf. He was gone, eaten up. There was only enough left of him that she would have to bury it to keep the buzzards and coyotes away.

She would come back to that chore. Meanwhile, she had to tend to the few creatures she had left. The cow was restless, would hardly give down her milk.

And when would she go dry? That was a question only waiting till Mary Dove got around to letting it be asked. She had been prepared to do without milk awhile, letting the calf get to be a bull; but now she might wait forever, before there was anything to quicken inside the old cow, and fill her udder again.

But when she wept burying the calf, it was not so much for what he might have become as for what he had been. That was another friend gone from her.

But she quickly turned back to the lambs; her thoughts were never far from them. She went and stood awhile looking from their pen to the brush arbor. She could have made that leap herself–certainly a great fierce panther could make it. She imagined how he might look. She knew a panther was a kind of cat, but she could not think he would be anything like a giant bobcat (the only cat she knew). She could only picture him as something like a huge, sleek, tawny coyote. She wondered–if she knew what the panther looked like, would her fear be more, or less?

There was no answer to that question, and no good in it

if there had been. All day she kept away from the only certainty, but when night drew near she went and loaded the gun.

The panther would be back that night. She knew it as clearly as if he had left a message for her with the lambs, and they had told her.

He would be back. He might come just at dusk, while there was still light enough for hunting, or he might wait until later, when the moon rose. She knew for sure that she must be waiting, ready to shoot, as close as she could get without keeping him away by the knowledge of her presence. She would have to get very close indeed, to be sure.

There was only one place for her to be. Within the shelter she had made for the lambs, back underneath the low brush roof. It came to her that she needed to be completely hidden, and she went up on the hill to cut some cedar boughs. She thought the smell of fresh cedar might cover up her human smell, too.

The chickens were not ready to go to roost when she decided it was time for her to hide herself, and she left them to take to their trees. The sun had not gone down. She would have a long time to be still and wait.

The lambs pushed all around her but at last got used to the fact that she was there. By good dark they had bedded down, asleep. The panther had not appeared.

She waited through the first hours of darkness, watching far pin points of stars, listening to pin points of sound: crickets, snapping of twigs, swishing of grass. Far away sounding, an owl called.

She had been afraid she might fall asleep, but she soon knew she need not have worried. Every part of her body seemed stretched as tight as the animal skins her father used to nail on his drying board, and the gun was a heavy cold weight against which she had unflaggingly to struggle.

She waited.

The sky lightened as the moon got ready to rise.

She knew there was something moving on the hillside. Whether she heard a faint sound or glimpsed a moving shadow she couldn't tell. Something was moving on the hillside. She barely breathed.

It came down, as she had foreseen, upon the roof of the brush arbor. She heard dried leaves of cedar crunching. She saw, or perhaps only felt, a shadow over the lamb pen. It could not have been a shadow; the moon was in the wrong part of the sky.

She raised the rifle, sighting against a faintly lighted sky. She could see the dark humped outline of the cedar-topped roof. It seemed to move.

An animal shape rose against the sky. It was not what she had thought. It was long and slim and moved like a snake. Something came up in her throat, turned her mouth sour. The shape moved closer. She fired the gun. The animal, snarling, sprang. Which happened first she never knew, but she could feel the moist breath of the beast upon her just before it fell heavily into the middle of the pen. The crying lambs crowded against her.

9

As soon as she could, when day came, she dragged the panther away, up onto a level, open hilltop where the buzzards would soon find it. It was a great heavy brute, but in life—for only a moment she had seen this—it had been graceful and lovely. Its skin was smooth to her touch, a pretty yellowish brown lit by the early sunshine. On the hill she stood and looked at it, wondering what exactly it was that she had killed.

Oh, she had killed the panther, and how surprised her father must be if he had any way to know. She had killed him because he was her enemy and she had to save her lambs. Not much else was left to her. Slowly, she went back down the hill.

There were the three hens, close together, scratching in

the dirt. Surely, surely, the rooster had not been carried off in the night by that prowling varmint she had forgotten when the panther screamed. But she sighed. If he had not, he would be. The hens would be. Three hens could not hold out long against so many enemies.

The cow mooed, still shut up in her pen. Mary Dove would go to her soon, to take the milk she was offering, and tell her the beast was dead that had killed her son and future mate. But that would not afford much comfort for the cow when she came to be in need of him.

Poor cow. Poor chickens. Poor Mary Dove. Only the lambs were not lonely. They might live on their silly, happy lives together until they made a great flock whitening the hillsides. And what good to her if they did? Yet of all her creatures she had loved them most and would again cradle the hateful gun in her arms, would shoot again the beautiful deadly beast, would give whatever had to be given to keep them alive around her.

They came bounding toward her, baaing some promise. She stood beholding them.

"What can you promise me, silly things?" she asked them, and they ran away again.

Mary Dove could find no true promise anywhere. When in fear and hatred she had raised her gun (not then feeling any dread of its cold hostility), she had believed, even against reason, that killing this enemy would save herself, her lambs —save all that was not already lost to her. But no, not true. There really was no promise.

The cow mooed again. "In just a little while," said Mary Dove, for heaviness held her.

A dove called from the creek, sitting perhaps on the dead hackberry limb that overhung the deep pool. The dove her sister called her, and she remembered that it had been many days since she had gone seeking the pool's old promise.

Surely it must be there still, but she was tired. She sat down, sighing, on the arbor bench.

"In a little while," she answered her sister.

II

Mary Dove and Red

In October the cowboy returned to the Badger Creek camp. The boss never blamed him for losing the cows in the spring, and picked him to stay there another season (for he knew the country) with a small herd Bar Diamond bought from a cattle company in central Texas.

He rode in late one warm day and found his sorry little old dugout still looking the same way it did when he left it. "Well, it ain't caved in," he said to himself. There was barely room in it for him to get in out of the weather to sleep, but for some reason this felt to him like coming home. He made a torch of dry grass and searched the place for snakes and spiders, without finding anything to worry him any. Some animal had been living there, but not lately; it didn't take him long to rake his floor clean. His coffeepot, tin cup, and rusty iron skillet were still in the corner where he had put them in the spring, when he left wondering if he ever would use them again.

He fixed himself a little supper and then rode out to locate the herd. He found it not far off, and was satisfied with the looks of it: he could go to bed. He didn't though. He had been riding for two days and had thought he was nearly exhausted, but he wasn't ready to go back to camp. It was nearly sundown now, and he looked out over a land of yellow-lit hilltops and misty blue hollows that somehow kept leading him on, making him ride farther than he needed to or meant to. It came to him how tired he had been of the Plains. "I shore do like this country," he said to himself, or his pony.

He wouldn't have had to come back. "It'll be lonesome down there," the boss said. "Maybe three years in a stretch is too much."

"I don't mind being lonesome," the cowboy said.

That wasn't exactly the truth, for there would be times when he did mind, he knew. He looked out around him now and reckoned that as far as he could see in every direction, there might not be another human being. Now that the sheep-man was dead. He wondered about Pardue's grave; he seemed to be riding towards it. Maybe it would be a kind of company for him in the lonesomest times.

Oh, he would get lonesome, but he had found out that in lots of ways he liked being by himself. Now he stopped and sat facing sundown, admiring the blazing west and the gold-lined, rosy little clouds floating high. If he had another man riding with him, he never would do that way. He liked that country, and he liked the sky above it, and it would suit him all right if he had it to himself for a while.

He rode on, thinking about some ideas he had. He was always figuring on ways he might get hold of some of that land sometime, get him a herd together—not so big he couldn't handle it himself, but big enough to make a living with. Then maybe spreading out some, later on, if he had some boys that took to the business. Because this idea had more to it than just him and the cows. It made him think of finding a woman somewhere (maybe one that would know why he took time to just sit still and watch clouds at sundown) and having kids that would grow up kind of thinking the way he did about things and learning to work alongside him, building up something they could have together.

He was coming to where he had buried Pardue. He hoped there hadn't anything dug up the grave. He thought if he found it all right he would come back some time and carve a name and date on the slab of rock he had used for a marker. Maybe there wouldn't anybody ever look for Pardue, or even know where in the world to look, but still he hated to think of a nameless grave.

He had no trouble finding it, and it was still undisturbed. He dismounted and stood with his hat off awhile. That was all he could think of to do.

The color was nearly gone from the sky now. He started riding homeward, but drifted east a little, watching for the moon to come up in a sky already whitened by it. He heard coyotes somewhere, an expected sound. Then he heard something else that caused him to stop still, straining to hear it again. It sounded like sheep. As he waited it came, faint but unmistakable: not any herd of sheep, just a little handful. He wondered if some new squatter had come in, or if it was possible that a few of Pardue's sheep had survived the blizzard. He would have thought that even if they had, the lobos or coyotes would have had them by now, or they would have drifted off that range. He thought if he didn't come across them accidentally somewhere, he would go and look for them someday when he didn't have anything better to do. If there was anybody living in that country, he wanted to know it.

For days the cowboy stayed busy around his camp. He had made up his mind (in case of another bad winter) to fix up a shelter for his pony Sangaree and the gray mare called Sissy that he had been using as a pack animal. He spent some time, too, extending his dugout and building a chimney so he could have a fire in times of rain or snow. He had made out all right before, but the spring blizzard had made him give a little more thought to things that might happen to men and animals not sufficiently protected from the weather.

It was hard to think of bad weather, though, in those bright warm days of late October. "It shore is a pretty fall," he often said to himself, or Sangaree or Sissy. He meant the light, dry air, the deep blue cloudless sky, the patches of rusty red, gold, and pale yellow along the creeks, most of all the feeling that he was where he belonged and would find there something he had been a long time looking for (was it just a piece of high level ground where you could think about building a house and barn some day, while you stood looking across the hazy hills and valleys?). He felt good. It was a pretty fall.

One day when he rode out to look at the cows he thought he heard the sheep again. They sounded farther away than before, and hushed as soon as he heard them, so that he asked himself whether he might not have been mistaken and it was some far-off bird hollering both times. But he was certain it didn't sound anything like a bird. He was about through with his camp work, and suddenly he knew he wanted a change.

"Let's go find them sheep," he said to Sangaree.

He circled around the head of Spring Creek and drifted east and south, riding slow, listening. He heard the sound again, not much closer. The sheep were moving, too, in about the same direction he was.

He kept riding east and a little south, down little draws and over hills, until he came to a running creek he knew but had never explored the full length of. He thought it might be at the head of that creek that Pardue's dugout was located, but as he had not foreseen welcome there he never had looked for it. The sheep (if any of Pardue's were left) might still be staying around the place, he supposed, but they must have been a good piece from it when he first heard them. He doubted that they would go back to the dugout so fast, and in fact they could now be nearly anywhere, in any direction. But since he didn't have anything else to go on, he thought he would follow that creek and see if it really was the one where the sheepherder had his diggings.

He rode along the creek, keeping on sloping hillsides so that he could watch down in the creek bed and look around him on the high ground too. He came in sight of a pretty spot: two or three big cottonwoods, growing close together, thrusting yellow-gold heads up against the blue; below them, a clump of bushy willows, softer yellow, like morning sunshine. The trees were so thick on that side of the creek that he could not see down into it, but he suspected they might be the sign of a good-sized hole of water. He climbed higher on the hill that rose steeply above the bunch of trees, thinking he might get located so as to see down into the creek better. Up there he could tell that there was a hole, all right, with the willows along one bank; but he could not tell much about the size and shape of it. The cottonwoods and some scrubby hackberries very nearly cut off his view. He wondered if his pony could get down to the water there, or if maybe he ought to get off and look around some on foot. He stopped on the hilltop, looking down. There was something white down there.

He dismounted, left Sangaree tied to a bush. He had to get closer to that water hole, get a look at whatever flashed so white. There never was a range sheep the color of what he saw; but by then he wasn't exactly looking for sheep. He had almost guessed–unbelievingly guessed–what it was he had glimpsed. He went slowly, having to be careful of his footing, over the edge of the high, steep bank. A few feet down he found a place where he could stand and see the water hole.

On the flat rock that formed the bank of the pool opposite him, with half a dozen sheep bunched around her, a young girl stood looking into the water. She was wearing some kind of loose-fitting white dress that barely covered her knees–that was the white thing. His foot slipped on a loose rock–he looked away from her, to make sure the bush he was grabbing for wasn't thorny. He barely knew she had lifted her face to him; there was no time to tell what it looked like. When he turned again she was already running (the sheep baaing, following her) along the creek bank that, above the round deep hole she had stood by, was flat and grassy. While he watched she disappeared around a bend in the creek.

He could not have moved fast enough from the precarious position he was in to run after her before she was lost from his sight. When later he thought of that moment (and countless times was he to think of it), he knew he could not have moved very fast anyhow. He stood there stunned–he did not know how long–with no space in his mind for anything except the picture that he could only have described as the prettiest thing he ever saw in his life. Like a many-colored sunset or reaching golden trees against the sky, it lifted him out of himself, shortened his breath, set his heart pounding.

That brown barefooted girl (she must have been out in the sun of every summer's day, was the cowboy's thought), that light-going, slim-looking figure of a girl with brown legs flashing below the short white dress, heavy braids of dark gleaming hair that bounced with her movements, the sheep around her running as if this were some game she played–what a picture, what a picture! But he had not seen her face. He tried and tried to bring that lifted blur of face into focus; but he had not seen it clearly, that was all. He felt unspeakably saddened by that fact, as though it meant a loss that could never be repaired.

All this was before, as he presently said to himself, he got his senses back. It was just a sunbrowned girl, that was all–member of some squatter family, no doubt, that had found the sheepman's dugout. As he made his way back to the bush where Sangaree waited, he thought of these things. There was nothing to get worked up about. Still, he would like to see her face, and find out what kind of folks she had. He guessed she would be one of a big family of children, the pitiful way she was dressed; but then he couldn't tell, she looked like she might be old enough to have a man of her own. Still, somehow–the way she ran with the sheep (and they were young, too, really still lambs)—he didn't think she was a married woman.

Well, he could see. He was pretty sure he could find the dugout; it couldn't be far off now.

He mounted his pony and rode up the creek, the way the girl had gone. Presently he heard the lambs, and could follow the sound of their baaing. Continuing along the creek as it formed a bend around a small rocky hill, he came to a clear spring bubbling out of sand rock. He looked to where the lambs called, up a slope about fifty feet from the spring. They were in a sorry-looking pen of willow stakes, close to a cedar-brush arbor that protected the entrance to a dugout. He didn't see any other livestock (though there were pens where Pardue must have kept some) or any further sign of any human being. He wondered if these sheep really could be the remnant of Pardue's herd, and who had penned them here. Well, there had to be somebody living with the girl, and she had to be somewhere. They didn't appear too anxious to be seen—hiding from the law, maybe—but he aimed to find out what he could about them.

He dismounted and got a drink, tied Sangaree near the spring, and went up the hill. He walked under the arbor—liking the smooth rock floor and the fresh cedar smell—and pounded on a heavy-looking door that opened into the rock-walled entrance way to the dugout. No response came, no sound at all.

He pounded and pounded, and shouted "Hey!" The lambs made the only sound. "I know you're in there," he shouted. "I ain't wanting nothing but just to say howdy."

But he never could rouse a soul.

"Well, I'll be back sometime when you're receiving," he finally called.

He guessed he would find out, sooner or later, who was living in Pardue's dugout. He would have plenty of time on his hands.

"Give us something to think about on them long winter nights, won't it, Sangaree?" he said as he rode slowly back to his camp.

2

When Mary Dove first found out the cattle were back–saw them darkening a far hillside as she wandered with the lambs –she felt afraid, and made up her mind not to get very far away from the dugout any more. But then she didn't see or hear them for a while, and never saw any sign of a man or a horse; so she began to think they had gone again, or moved so far away from her she didn't need to worry.

So she grew careless and let the fall weather call her out on the hills, let the lambs lure her, for they delighted now in seeking farther pastures. One day she felt they were moving toward the deep creek where her father and his herd had died, and she thought, Maybe I would like to look at it again.

But then, when she came in sight of the round hill that stood near the head of that creek, she saw cows grazing near the foot of it, and she turned her lambs around. They were cross, and baaed at her; she took a stick and drove them, until they made up their minds to follow where she led. She was not much afraid that time–she had still seen no sign of a horseman–but she thought she ought to stay nearer home.

The weather was the warmest it had been in many days. She got so hot and sweaty hurrying across the hills homeward that she thought of going swimming in the pool. There was no idea in her mind of anything more than a bath to cool and cleanse her sticky body, and she wondered if it mightn't be a little cold for that, down in the round pool. She went there, the lambs now coming consentingly with her, and stood on the rock looking down into the water.

She heard a noise above her, raised her eyes, and he was

there. She saw only dark clothes and a black hat on the figure of a man, but she knew at once it was the rider she had seen in the spring near the place where the sheep died. She had not been as much afraid of the panther poised above her: fear tingled in her arms and shoulders, drew the strength from her legs. For an instant she felt she could not move; then a surge of power came through her and she ran to her dugout like a rabbit to its hole. Seeing no one behind her, she paused to put the lambs in their pen (not thinking why, but somehow for their safety), then hurled herself into the dugout and bolted the door with the heavy iron bar her father had brought from town so long before and never known a need for.

She lay panting in the dark, waiting. At last there came a pounding on the door, and then shouting. After a long time she knew the man had gone away, but not before she heard him say he would be back.

When the panther came, unknown and fearful as he was to her, she had guessed at what he might do and fought successfully against him. But she could not any way imagine what to expect of a man. She could not even guess what terrible things he might do, having only her father's vague warning to guide her.

The man would be back: how many days would pass, what time of day or night he might appear, she could not know, but she must never forget to watch for him. She loaded the gun and kept it near her. She tried never to go farther away from the dugout than the spring. She had decided to let the cow wander free in the daytime, finding the best pasture and maybe sometime (for this was one thing Mary Dove had thought of when she saw the range cows were back) a bull to mate with. But now she tied the cow near the spring every day, not wanting to take the risk of having to go and look for her. She watched the lambs all day, and penned them early. The three hens had learned to roost in the dugout, and like them Mary Dove went to bed every night at the first sign of failing light.

Though the nights were cool and she needed a fire in the dugout, the days stayed warm and clear. Mary Dove spent most of her daylight hours sitting on the rocks at the edge of the brush arbor. She shucked her harvested corn, and threshed her dried beans, but she never stayed long with the tasks she found to do. She was watching and waiting.

One day the bluebirds came. Every fall they would come to the creek and stay awhile–Mary Dove had learned from her father that they were on their way south for the winter. This year she had not thought to look for them, and when they came–when the flock descended around her like falling bits of summer sky–she felt the cold dread that possessed her washed out of her breast by rising waves of long-forgotten joy.

She loved the bluebirds. "They're the sign of happy times," her father once had said, and it always seemed to Mary Dove that this was true, for it made her happy just to look at them. Among the bluebirds she never was seized with the unfulfillable yearning she sometimes knew, or visited with the sense of an unexplainable force. These birds of soft clear blue, with their gentle, friendly ways, simply filled her with a warm content. She could sit still and watch them for hours, and they would come right up to her. Birds were never very shy of Mary Dove but she had often thought the bluebirds were the friendliest of all.

She slowly stretched out a hand toward one bird that had landed near her on the grass. Curious, it moved close. She almost dared wonder if it would hop on into her open hand, as she had often wished a bird would do.

Suddenly, as if Mary Dove had made some quick movement, it flew away. The whole flock rose with a flutter and disappeared.

Fear came swiftly back to Mary Dove. She guessed what had scared the birds away. Even before she looked and saw him, she reached for the rifle that lay on the rocks nearby, and as she lifted her eyes she raised the gun and looked at him along the barrel of it.

"Now don't shoot me," he said. "I'm sorry I scared off the birds."

"You stop," she said. "Don't you come no closer."

He stopped. But he grinned at her. He had a one-sided grin like one long known to her. He had a soft voice, too, a kind-sounding voice like her father's. Doubt came and tempted her, but she cast her mind back to her father's stern warnings. He had worn no grin when he told her what to do about a man, nor had his voice been soft.

"I just wanted to get acquainted," the man said. "I'm your neighbor–got a cow camp a few miles over yonder." He pointed southwest.

Mary Dove did not move or answer.

"Where's your menfolks?" he asked.

Instinctively, she knew that was a question not to be answered.

"Get away," she said.

"Now I ain't gonna hurt you," he said, "and I don't want to know nothing about you that you don't want to tell." He came a step closer.

"Stop right now," she said, "or I'll shoot."

"You wouldn't," he said.

He was so nearly right. She believed what he said–or nearly. But she had been afraid so long. And wasn't it a law of God to do what your father said?

She trembled, looking into his smiling blue eyes. It would have been easier if he had been preparing to pounce, like the panther, or striking, like the snake. The rifle barrel dropped, a little.

"I knew you wouldn't," he said, taking another step towards her.

"I have to," she said, and with a terrible struggle to hold the gun steady, she fired.

Bleeding, he fell to the ground.

"You're hurt bad!" she cried, and hurried to where he lay.

3

Later he thought he must have fainted from losing blood. His leg hurt like the devil, but he had known pain before, and stood it. The last thing he saw was the girl bending over him. Her face, clear at last.

The first time he saw her, her face had been turned away from him and he never got a chance to look at it before she ran away. Then he had seen it partly hidden behind a great long gun, and he still didn't know what she looked like. Only at the last, just before he lost consciousness, it came clear and close before him, like a mother's face coming down to kiss an ailing child.

Dark hair drawn back from a smooth, broad forehead. Dark eyes, full of sympathy and unshed tears. High cheekbones and flat cheeks–a look he liked (high-class, was the way he thought of it). Soft lips, trembling.

He had tried many times to imagine a face pretty enough to belong to the slim brown girl running lightly with her lambs, but he never in a hundred years could have thought up one as good as the true one that she bent to him as he lay wounded on the ground.

When everything that had happened started coming clear to him, he had the feeling that he must have lain for days (on the thin mattress under the brush arbor where he now found himself) feverishly dreaming of that face. He even wondered if the face was real.

He saw dried-out cedar overhead and knew where he was, but not how he got there. He turned his head and saw the sheep (seven of them, he now counted) grazing close by. When he moved they looked curiously at him but did not seem disturbed. He wondered where the girl was.

Was there a girl? He felt his stiff, sore thigh, wrapped up in some kind of bandage, and he grinned. Yes, there was this girl all right, that had put a rifle bullet in him and then come running to nurse him and make him a bed. So he guessed, for he hadn't seen a sign of anybody else, even in his dreams. Her folks must be gone somewhere. She had nursed him all right. Good Lord, he suddenly thought, did she take my britches off? He pushed back the blanket that covered him and painfully sat up. She hadn't taken his britches off, but she–or somebody–had carefully cut off the leg of his britches and his underwear, too, leaving his leg bare and his wound wrapped up in what seemed to be strips of an old cotton shirt.

There was a girl, and was it really her face he so clearly remembered?

"Hey!" he called.

He heard a door creak, the dugout door. She was coming. He was watching for her as though his life depended on seeing what she looked like.

There was a bench close to his bed. He thought she must have been sitting on it a lot; for some reason he expected her to come there now, and was looking there for her, wanting to see her as he thought he must have been seeing her for days.

She came slowly, her bare feet making no sound on the rock floor, and sat lightly on the edge of the bench at the end farthest from him. She looked the way he thought she did: graceful and slender, as she had been among the lambs; gentle and soft, as when he watched her reaching out toward the bluebird. She reminded him now of that bluebird–having come just so close and perched so lightly that she seemed about to fly away. She sat facing him, her lips a little apart, her eyes wide and wondering.

"Don't fly off," he said.

She settled back a little on the bench. "Do you want something?" she asked.

"I want a lot of things," he said. "I reckon the main thing I want is to find out why you thought you had to shoot me."

"Because," she said, "Papa told me that's what I must do."

"Why don't your papa do his own shooting?"

"He's dead," she said.

The explanation came to him then, but he couldn't believe it. "What folks have you got?" he asked her.

"I ain't got none," she said. "I just had Papa, and he's gone."

"Dead."

Mary Dove had believed she wouldn't talk to this man, would tell him nothing, make him go away as soon as his leg got well enough for him to ride his horse. But then, he wasn't what she had thought he would be. Whether she could possibly shoot him again, even threaten to shoot him again, she couldn't tell. Now, just the way he said that one word–*dead*–made him sound like somebody that cared what happened to people. She couldn't, somehow, make herself believe he wouldn't be as kind a man to her as her father had been. He made her realize how much she wanted to tell what had happened to her father and how it had been for her living by herself–living so long without anybody to tell anything to.

"He's gone," she said. "I never seen him dead, but I know he must be."

"How long has he been gone?"

"He went off in the snow last spring, and the sheep died, too, and I reckon he's buried underneath 'em."

"What was his name?"

"Name?" she said.

"He had a name, didn't he?"

"Oh I'm silly," she said. "Of course he had a name, but it's been a long time since I thought about it because he was always just Papa to me."

"Well, was it Pardue?"

"Tom Pardue. Yes, that was his name."

"And what's your name, then?"

"Mary Dove."

"Mary Dove Pardue."

"I reckon. But Mary Dove is all he ever called me."

"Well, Mary Dove, I reckon names ain't so important. But

I knowed a man named Pardue–a tall lean fellow with half-gray hair and a droopy mustache."

She moved along the bench closer to him, her eyes fixed on his face. "That was Papa," she whispered.

"Then he's dead. I seen him a few times living, and I seen him dead. I buried him."

She leaned forward over the wounded man. He could see her eyes fill up with tears. "Tell me," she said.

He told her what he had found after the blizzard, what he had done. He let her cry silently a little while then. At last she looked up, wiping her face with her hand, and spoke.

"I think I seen you that day," she said.

"You seen me, and you was all by yourself, and yet you let me go?"

"I was afraid," she said. "Papa said never let no man come near, and I was afraid."

"Don't be afraid of me, Mary Dove. Do you want to know my name?"

Still teary-eyed, she nodded. "What to call you," she said.

"Call me Red," he said.

"Red?" she said. "Is that really a name for a man?"

He grinned at her. "No, it's not really," he said. "My folks named me Christopher Columbus, and my last name's Jones–I reckon you can guess why I've just about forgot I ever had any name but Red."

She studied him seriously. "No," she said.

He shook his head. "You're a funny girl," he said. "You do see why they call me Red, don't you?"

"No," she said.

"If I'as in the sun you would. I don't reckon there's ever been anybody with hair redder than mine."

"It don't look red to me," she said. "It ain't like a redbird or a woodpecker's head."

"Oh Mary Dove," he said, "you don't know nothing. If it don't look red to you, what does it look like?"

Again she studied him. "It looks to me," she said at last, "the color of clouds in the west when the sun's going down."

"Well, that sounds pretty," he said, "but I reckon most folks would say it's just plain red. Didn't you ever see a redheaded person before?"

She looked at him in a wondering way; it was a while before she answered. "I don't remember," she finally said, "ever seeing any person in the world but my papa."

"Not anybody a-tall?" he cried, amazed.

"Some Indians come by once," she said, "but I didn't hardly see them. Papa wouldn't let me out."

Then he looked at her awhile. "Good Lord," he said at last, half under his breath, then went on in the half-joking way he had been talking: "Well, I ain't gonna ask you no more about that, not right now. At least we've made ourselves acquainted."

"Have we?" she said.

"Yes," he said, "but we'll make it proper. Mary Dove Pardue, meet Christopher Columbus Red Jones."

He held out his hand, to be shaken. She took it in both of hers.

He let her hold it a moment, then put it slowly down. "Someday," he said, "I'll teach you how to shake hands. Now there's some more things you've got to tell me."

She folded her hands in her lap and waited.

"First–how long have I been here?"

She looked surprised. "It was yesterday I shot you," she said.

"It seems so long."

"You had fever, I think. You twisted around and talked a lot. I thought you was asleep. I washed you a lot with spring water."

"You're a good nurse," he said. "How come you know so well how to take care of me?"

"Papa got hurt bad once," she said, "in a accident with a horse. And sometimes I took care of animals. He told me things to do."

"Well, I'm glad of that," he said, "and I thank you for taking care of me. I reckon you had to shoot me for some reason, but you didn't have to nurse me after you done it."

"You don't know why I had to shoot you," she said.

"No," he said, "I can't say I understand that."

"It was Papa," she said. She explained about how her father brought the gun and said she must use it to keep any man from ever coming into their dugout. "I had to do what Papa said," she told him, "because that's a law of God."

"Well–yes," he answered. "But there's one of them that says thou shalt not kill, too."

"He told me about that," she said. "But he said there was times when it didn't apply."

"I expect he was right," Red said. "And I guess I don't blame you for shooting me, but I wish you wouldn't do it any more."

She looked thoughtful. "I don't think I will," she said slowly. "I don't believe you can be the kind of a man my papa feared might come."

"I hope I'm not," he said.

4

Red didn't think his leg was going to bother him a whole lot, but when he tried getting up later that day he could tell he wouldn't be getting very far away from that dugout for a while. Mary Dove unwrapped his wound and washed it with cool fresh water. It had bled when he got up.

"You mustn't get up," she said. "I can clean up the bed when I need to, and you could put on some of Papa's clothes."

She would look after him the way she would a sick sheep, he realized, and not be bothered a bit more by the messiness. She was a very unusual girl.

He had a lot of things about that girl that he wanted to try to think out, but for a good while his leg hurt too much.

Then when the pain let up a little he went to sleep, and when he woke up he remembered that he hadn't given any thought yet to the job he was supposed to be doing and the shape things might be in at his own dugout.

"Hey Mary Dove!" he called.

She came quickly.

"Set down," he said.

She sat on the bench, at home there now.

"Listen," he said, "I got to talk to you."

"All right," she said.

"It looks like I'm gonna have to stay here for a while."

"Yes."

"Well–you reckon you can ride my horse?"

"I reckon. I rode Papa's horse."

"You reckon you could find my dugout, if I told you where it was?"

"I can find it," she said. "What do you want me to do there?"

He guessed you didn't need to do much leading up to things with Mary Dove. Or any beating around the bush. He told her what he wanted her to do: see if the herd was still grazing by the round hill on Spring Creek; go by there and on to his camp (he told her the way to go), catch his gray mare and load up his grub and bed roll and everything, and bring it all back to the dugout. He couldn't tell when he would be going back.

"Can you do all that?" he asked.

"Yes," she said. "I'll go in the morning."

Next morning she brought him a fried egg and a bowl of milky mush for breakfast, then put a dipper and bucket of fresh water beside him, and a hunk of cornbread wrapped in a clean rag.

"It'll be something to eat if you get hungry while I'm gone," she said. "I'll fix something better when I get back."

He watched her put the lambs in the pen to keep them from following her, then go around to the pen where she had put

Sangaree. She was wearing a pair of her father's trousers, cut off, and she rode off a-straddle, handling the pony with ease.

It took her nearly all day to make the trip. He wasn't hurting so much and he slept a lot, but between naps he had plenty of time to think and wonder about Mary Dove and Pardue.

The man he had buried was her father–there could be no doubt of that. She had told Red her mother was dead and she couldn't remember anything about her ways or what she looked like. Here in this dugout there had never been anybody but Mary Dove and her father, and all she could clearly remember was her life there. What Red couldn't figure out (what he asked himself a dozen times or more that day) was why Pardue had kept her a secret. Why had he let Red think he lived by himself? Why hadn't Mary Dove ever been anywhere, or seen anybody? What in the world would make a man want to raise a girl that way? He wondered what Pardue had thought would ever become of her, for although the man seemed to have done everything he could to show his daughter how to protect herself against intruders, he must have known that sometime she would need more than just a way to keep strange men from coming near.

When Red thought about Mary Dove by herself there all the months since her father died, the way she had to do, he felt so bad he couldn't keep from shedding a few tears. (But of course he was weak from being hurt, he told himself.) The little thing was so pitiful, and didn't even seem to know how pitiful she was–her thinking she could go on living there always, taking care of herself without any help.

Before she got back he was beginning to worry about her. He never should have asked her to go. Even if she had grown up in that country, he didn't think she had ever been so far away from the dugout before. She could get lost–no telling what might happen to her out there lost in the hills in the night.

But she got home before sundown. She rode up close to

where he lay under the arbor and dismounted, to stand near him a little bit.

"Are you all right?" she asked him.

"I'm fine," he said. "I was worried about you."

"Why?" she said.

"I don't know," he said. "I thought maybe you had trouble. Did you find the cows all right?"

"They'as where you said," she told him. "I looked a little for Papa's grave, but I couldn't find it. I might be a little bit late on that account."

"It don't matter," he said. "I'll take you there some time. Did you get everything?"

"Everything you said, I think."

She unloaded the mare and set the stuff down by the dugout door.

"I'll go and put the horses in the pen," she told him. "There's a bank in the north, looks like we're fixing to have some weather."

She was soon back, saying, "Now we've got to get you down in the dugout."

"Does it look pretty bad?" he asked her.

"I reckon it'll rain," she said, "and seems like it's time we can look for a cold spell."

"It is," he agreed. "But we ain't had nothing but pretty weather all fall, so I guess we can't grumble."

He was trying to get up. She hurried and bent to help him.

"Just lean on me," she said, "and maybe it won't be too bad."

"It ain't bad," he said, gritting his teeth. "You're too little for me to lean on."

"No I'm not, I'm strong," she said. "You lean on me."

He found he had to, a little. He guessed he was nearly a foot taller than she was, and no telling how much more he weighed. But he put his arm across her shoulders and let her help him. They got him into the dugout that way, and she helped him get down onto the bed that was made up in one corner.

"This is your bed," he said.

"I'll get the other one, move it back down here," she said. She said she had to go and milk, and get some wood in, and see about the lambs, and then she would come and cook them something good for supper. "Looks like you've got some good stuff," she said. "Can I fry some salt pork?"

"Fix anything you can find," he said. "I'm hungry too."

After she was gone he got to wondering what she had been having to eat. Lord, he thought, I'm nearly glad I come and let her shoot me.

5

Rain came that night, and for a week or more the weather stayed cold and damp. Mary Dove never saw a trace of ice anywhere, but doing her outside work she would get to feeling chilled all through her body. She began wearing an old sheepskin jacket her father had made for himself, because her own coat was too skimpy to protect her. She tried to wear a pair of his old worn-out shoes, but they were so much too big she couldn't get around in them, so she kept going barefooted.

When she came in she would pile more wood on the fire and sit on a bench in front of it holding her feet up close to the flames.

Red, lying on his hard bed in a dim corner of the dugout, would watch her sometimes, slim and dark against the bright firelight like a black-paper cutout of the princess in some fairy tale. He slept a lot in those days, and his leg still hurt whenever he moved. He didn't think much, and when he did he was often wondering how long he would be there, what would happen to the cows, whether there was any way he could get word to the boss if he didn't get well in a hurry.

For these reasons (or so he explained to himself later, when he was feeling ashamed of himself) he let several days go by before he noticed anything much about Mary Dove except what a pretty picture she made by the fire, with her slim ankles lifted. Besides, it was always so dim in the dugout, even with a big fire going, he couldn't tell much about what she was wearing anyway.

Then one day she came in and, stopping to hang her stinking sheepskin coat on a peg in the wall, brought a bucket she was carrying to show him what she had for their dinner.

"See," she said. "Quails. Dressed and ready to cook. The trap was just full of them this morning."

Her white cotton skirt where it had hung below the sheepskin coat was dripping and muddy. That was what met his eyes first when, hearing her coming, he turned toward her. She ought to have better clothes, at least for the winter; he had thought that before. His glance slipped down along her wet shiny legs—they were bare, her feet were bare. Her feet were wet and mud-splattered, and on one foot he could see a twig of grass stuck between two toes.

He hadn't looked at the bucket of birds. "Don't you like quail?" she asked. He barely heard her, did not answer.

"Mary Dove," he said. He spoke roughly. "Mary Dove, tell me, haven't you even got any shoes?"

She bent to pick up the bucket, turned away from him to the bench where she got her food ready to cook. "No," she said, in a voice thick with tears.

Then it came to him what she had asked about the quails—he guessed he had hurt her feelings. "I like quail," he said. "It sure will taste good."

She didn't answer. In a minute she sat down by the fire and began wiping her feet and legs with what looked like an old rag. Then, in her usual way, she began to warm her feet. She kept her back to him.

"Mary Dove," he said, "I'm plum crazy. I ought to have knowed you wouldn't have any shoes."

She turned towards him. He lay only a few feet away.

"I've got shoes," she said. "They ain't wore out. But I growed so much last year I can't get 'em on. Papa would have got me some at town if he'd a been here. And I tried to wear some of his, but they won't stay on."

"And I reckon you ain't got no warm clothes you can wear, either," he said.

"I had some of these things," she said, fingering her wet, muddy shift. "I reckon they'as supposed to be nightgowns; but they'as the only things I had that was made full enough so as I could wear 'em. I reckon I can't wear them much longer, but I've got some clothes, I think, if I could get my mama's trunk open."

She had to tell him about the trunk. "I know I could get it open somehow," she finished, "but I hated to ruin it, and lately I reckon I sort of forgot, or thought it'd bother you, or something."

"Where is it?" he said. "I'll help you get it open."

She pointed to the corner where it stood.

"I reckon I kind of hate to open it, in a way," she said. "Seems like I'll be doing something to my mama–I don't know what, that's silly I know."

"Your mama'd be glad to know you was getting some clothes to wear, I imagine," he said. "What all do you reckon's in it?"

"Just dresses, was what Papa said. I thought there might be some shoes, but I don't know."

"Reckon you could move it over here?" he said. "Is it very heavy?"

"I don't know," she said. "I'll see."

She moved the pile of bedclothes, and tugged at the handle on one end of the trunk. It wasn't very heavy. She scooted it across the floor.

He sat up on his bed and examined the lock. "I believe I could pick that," he said. "Could you find me a piece of wire somewheres?"

"There's some baling wire at the cowshed," she said, and went and fetched it.

He worked awhile, not getting the lock to move, then laid the wire down. "Seems like I get tired easy," he said. "I'll wait a little bit and try again."

"I guess there's other ways," she said.

"I could take the lock off," he said.

"Well," she said.

In a few minutes he picked up the wire and turned back to the lock. "Mary Dove," he said, "don't you know anything at all about your mama?"

"Papa couldn't hardly stand to talk about her, seemed like," Mary Dove said. "He said she was a good woman. He said there wasn't very many good women in the world, as far as he could tell, but she was one of 'em. He said that was all I needed to know, and if I could be just like her he wouldn't ask for nothing else."

She paused, watching him a little while. "But I never did know," she added, "what he meant by that. I wouldn't know if I was a good woman or not."

"I reckon you're just naturally good, Mary Dove," Red said, "–if you did shoot me. You've been good to me since."

She didn't know of anything to say to that. She waited.

"We'll have to pry it open," he said at last. "Have you got a crowbar?"

"No," she said, "I don't think so. A hammer?"

"Maybe," he said.

She got the hammer. "I can do that," she said. "I just didn't think how to do, I guess I hated to think about it."

He let her, for he was feeling tired again. She tested a few times, to see how much strength it would take. When it came off, she fell back a little, but caught herself. "Well," she said.

"Well, open it," he said.

He was hoping for something more than dresses, he knew that. For Mary Dove's sake, he said to himself. A girl ought to know more than she did about who her mother and father had been.

She put back the trunk lid and began taking out dresses, holding them up before her. They were just the kind of dresses he was used to seeing women wear—dark calico, one brown one that looked like wool, petticoats too. They would be all right for her to wear—maybe a little big, but big enough: that was the main thing.

Then: "Here's some shoes!" she cried.

But the shoes wouldn't begin to go on her feet, they soon saw.

"They're not any bigger than my year-before-last ones," Mary Dove said sadly.

"Is that all?" Red asked.

"There's something," she said. "Wrapped up in a white sheet, it looks like."

"Her wedding dress, maybe," he said.

She straightened up from the trunk and looked at him. "Wedding dress?" she said.

He was always forgetting all the things Mary Dove didn't know. "To wear when she married your papa," he said. "Girls allus likes to have pretty dresses to get married in."

"Oh," she said doubtfully. He wondered what else it was she didn't understand.

"See what it is," he said.

She bent and opened up the folded sheet. "Ahhhh," she let out her breath. She lifted the dress, held it—as she had done the others—in front of her.

"Is it a wedding dress?" she asked him.

He had seen things like that but not at a wedding. Bright blue silk was what it looked like, with black lace and silver things trimming the waist and ruffles around the skirt. It shore comes down low in the front, Red thought. The skirt seemed short, too.

"Is it?" she asked again.

"Not a wedding dress, I don't think," Red told her. "I guess it's what you call a party dress–you might wear it just to dance and have a good time in."

He thought she was going to ask him some questions about that, but at last she just said "Oh" and folded the dress and put it back in the trunk. "I may not ever wear that un," she said. "It shore is pretty though."

"You could try it on some time," he said. "Put on one of the others now, I'll cover up my head."

She picked a dark red calico and put the rest back in the trunk. The dress was cut to button down the front, below the waist, and went on easily. When she buttoned it up she found it was still loose–maybe it was supposed to be.

"Look," she said.

She stood before him and he uncovered his eyes. "It's just fine," he said, "and you can grow into it some–if you're fixing to grow any more, which I doubt." He studied her a minute. "You know," he said, "if you'd pin them long plaits up around your head, like womenfolks do, you wouldn't look anything like a little girl."

She looked puzzled, then smiled. "Oh I've got some hairpins Papa brought me one time," she said. "Is that what they're for?"

He showed her how to put up her hair; the coronet of thick braids made her look tall and womanly.

He looked her up and down. "By golly, I'll *make* you some shoes," he said.

After dinner, all the rest of that day, he worked on the shoes, using what he could of her father's worn-out pair and an old sheepskin she found for him, calling her sometimes to measure her foot against what he had completed. He worked a good while sitting on the edge of the bench, near the fire where he could see better. He said he felt better sitting up, it didn't bother his thigh when he sat this way; but after a time he went back and eased himself down onto the bed.

Mary Dove was busy too. After one trip out in the wet she

had decided to hem up her dresses a little, high enough to keep the skirts from being ruined as they swept the ground.

She sat trying to think about the way her mother might have been, wearing the dresses. What did women do, living in houses, being in towns full of things they could buy? What would they be doing when they put on a thing like the shiny, glittering dress in the bottom of the trunk?

She wondered whether Red would tell her if she asked him. "He knows," she thought. "He knows everything that Papa did, or even more, and maybe wouldn't tell me I'd be better off not knowing." But often her father hadn't wanted her to talk to him if he was working, or felt tired or sick. She quietly stitched up her hems.

From time to time, Red put down his work and shifted his weight to rest his wounded thigh. He looked at Mary Dove working, thought he'd never seen so quiet a girl or woman in his life.

"I guess you got out of the habit of talking," he said to her.

She looked up from her work. "Do you want to talk?" she asked him.

"I feel like it today," he said.

"Then I wish you'd tell me things," she said.

"What kind of things, Mary Dove?"

"Where you lived before this, what you done–"

"Well–"

"Have you got a mother?"

"Oh I've got a mother," he said. "And five sisters, too."

"Ahhh," she breathed.

"You think that sounds good, do you?"

"Ain't it, Red?"

"Pretty good," he said. "But sometimes it felt kind of like living in a dugout full of chickens."

"You got to quit minding my old hens," she said. "I told you why they've got to roost with us."

"I'm gonna build you a coop for 'em, soon as I can get out of here."

"But you couldn't do that about your sisters."

"That's the truth," he said. "And I reckon that's the reason I left home."

"Tell me," she said, "about home."

He brought it before him and tried to show her. He put down his work and looked into the flickering dugout dimness.

"We had a big old house," he said. "Ten rooms, all about twice as big as this dugout. Some was upstairs, a second floor on top of the first one, and steps going up, like the dugout steps. A porch all the way across the front, kind of like the brush arbor, only part of the house, built out of wood like the house was."

He stopped and looked at her. "Go on," she said.

"I kind of think your pa must've had a house like that in mind when he built the brush arbor–must've lived in one somewheres. There's lots of houses like that back east; could be you was born in one of them.

"But it was a sorry old house, there's lots of 'em sorry, too. Ours I don't reckon had been painted since before the War. Everything falling apart, no money to get it fixed up. Before the War, Pa had a lot of land and niggers to work it. But then they freed the niggers and he lost the land, and pretty soon he died from a hurt he got in the War."

He could tell she was wondering about something he said. "What is it you don't understand about that?" he asked her. "War?"

"I heard of war," she said. "Papa used to sing a song about it."

"Oh Mary Dove," Red said then, "didn't you ever hear tell of a nigger?"

So he had to try to tell her what a Negro was. Black, he said. Not anything like white folks, not any way. They came from a place called Africa, far across the sea, where the most of the Negroes still lived, wild savages in the jungle.

"What made 'em leave their homes, Red?" Mary Dove asked him.

"White folks brought 'em," he said, "to work for them. The niggers was slaves, before the War. A white man would own a nigger and look after 'im, give 'im plenty to eat and a place to live, and the nigger done whatever work the white man needed done."

"Ain't that so, any more?"

"No, the slaves was took away from their rightful owners. There ain't no slaves no more."

"Did they get to go back home?"

"No, they'as too many of 'em. Now they just got to work if they get a chance, and they live off to theirselves, because of course they can't mix with white folks. They're lucky if they get to be servants in some white family, because then they generally get a decent place to live. But they don't half know how to take care of theirselves–they was better off when they was slaves."

"Don't seem like it could be better, being owned like a cow or a sheep. I wouldn't like to be."

"Well, they ain't like white folks," Red said.

She looked at him as though she wanted to ask another question, but at last sighed and said, "There's so much I don't know, and never will I guess. Now go on and tell about the sisters."

Listening, she seemed to see a house full of sisters, laughing, singing, spilling out onto the porch in white dresses when their sweethearts came to call. One of them married before Red left home, and her wedding dress was rosy pink silk.

"Not like the dress in my mama's trunk," she said.

"No, not like that."

"Did they have dresses like that?"

"Not much like that."

"Why not?"

"Oh–lots of reasons."

"What would a reason be?"

"Well, one reason might be"–he carefully said–"not having much money. They never had half the dresses they thought they wanted." He paused, remembering he used to say that, teasing them, but it wasn't wholly true. "But then," he added, "my sisters is good girls. I don't want to make 'em sound too silly. They made their own dresses and helped my mother lots of ways. She sews for the public, and they do what they can to help out. I used to think sometimes they'd drive me crazy, but the truth is I wouldn't trade a one of them for anything."

"You left home because of them?"

"Not really. Or in a way. I had to get out and try to make a living, get money to send home and help my mother finish raising them. They wouldn't believe how much I miss 'em sometimes."

"I used to think about having a sister," Mary Dove said. "I wish I could see them someday."

"Maybe you can, someday," Red said to her.

They thought their own thoughts for a while, not saying any more about that.

Then he said, "Come here, Mary Dove, and try on your shoes."

She went and put them on, tied them with leather thongs he had made, walked around the dugout, firmly and freely as she walked outdoors. They felt good, she could wear them.

He watched her, remembering his sisters stepping little steps in shiny tight shoes. "They ain't so bad," he said. "Now don't say I never give you nothing."

"What?" she said.

"It's just a saying," he said. "It means I'm giving you a present."

"Why would you give me a present?" she said.

"Oh, I guess–for shooting me."

She put her hands to her face. "Don't tease me, Red," she said, in a sobbing voice. "I *wish* I hadn't done that."

He limped to where she stood, gently took her hands in his, and gave her a kiss on the cheek, quick as a kiss for a sister. "Don't cry," he said. "I really don't care if you did."

6

That night, after Mary Dove had done her outside work and prepared their usual supper of milk and mush, she said to Red, "I got a surprise for you."

She took her guitar from the corner where she kept it, wrapped in an old blanket to protect it from the damp, and sat down with it on the bench by the fire.

Red was lying on his bed. He lifted himself on one elbow. "Hey, a git-tar," he exclaimed.

"I'm fixing to sing you something," she said, "on account of the present you give me."

She cradled the guitar in her arms, loving it, bringing forth from it sounds that predicted a sweet, sad song. She sang:

"Oh who's gonna shoe your pretty little foot,
And who's gonna glove your hand,
Who's gonna kiss your red ruby lips
When I'm gone to a far-off land?"

She looked up and laughed. "I just remembered that song today," she said. "But"—she held up a foot in the thick bulky shoe Red had made—"ain't nobody gonna call that a pretty little foot."

"Not little, maybe," Red admitted. "But go on—sing another verse."

"I'll sing the answer," she said.

"Papa's gonna shoe my pretty little foot,
Mama's gonna glove my hand,
Sister's gonna kiss my red ruby lips,
For I won't have no man."

She stopped singing and absently strummed the guitar.

"I used to worry about that, you know," she said. "I knew my mama was dead, but when I was a little tiny thing I never could understand why I didn't have no sister."

"Well, give me the git-tar," Red said, "and I'll sing it to you another way."

She handed the guitar to him where he now sat on the edge of his mattress.

"Do you care if I tune it different?" he asked.

"No," she said, "I tune it all kinds of ways."

When the strings sounded right to him he strummed a chord and then sang to her:

"Red's gonna shoe your pretty little foot,
Red's gonna glove your hand,
And Red's gonna kiss your red ruby lips,
'Cause you done got a man!"

Mary Dove clapped her hands and laughed like a little child. "Oh Red," she cried. "You made up a good un."

"What if I meant it?" he asked.

"Well," she said, and bent to him. He kissed her lightly on the lips. "We can play like you're my man," she said. "Now sing me another verse of that song."

"Yes, I'd better," he said. (Before he decided to teach her what kissing really was.) He sang:

"Oh don't you see that lonesome dove
A-flying from vine to vine,
A-mourning for his long-lost love
As I must mourn for mine."

She was tickled at that. "Oh I was a lonesome dove all right, when you come," she said. "But Papa never sung that verse, I didn't know it was part of the song."

"Folks don't all sing it alike," he said. "Do you know this verse?"

He sang one that started, "The blackest crow that ever flew will surely turn snow white," and she joined him. They sang all they knew of that song together.

"Yes, I was sure enough lonesome," she said, "and now here we are playing and singing together, and it don't hardly seem real. Seems like it's something I just made up in my mind, or dreamed about. I wonder if you'll be gone when I wake up in the morning."

"I won't be," he said shortly.

She didn't say anything to that. She wished she hadn't mentioned his going that way, for of course he would go when he was well. His life called him a different way; hers was right here. He would go back to his sisters; she would stay–with hers? She thought of telling him the silly thing about thinking a dove was her sister, but it was not a time she wanted him to laugh at her.

"Let's sing some more songs," she said.

They discovered there were a good many songs they both knew, but he knew so many more than she did, he was always asking, "Do you know this un?" and then he'd have to sing it by himself.

"Oh you know so many songs," Mary Dove said. "I wish I could learn 'em every one, for if I knew all them songs to sing I don't think I'd ever get lonesome a-tall. How come you know so many?"

"Back home," he said, "we'as what they called a singing family. Seems like we'as born knowing songs."

"I bet your sisters sing pretty."

"They're good singers all right," he said. "Sunday mornings, you can't hardly hear anybody but them in the church house."

"Church house?" she said.

"Oh Mary Dove," he said.

"I guess," she said, "it's something else that Papa never told me."

"He told you about God. Didn't he ever say a word about going to church?"

She shook her head. "He never told me very much about God," she said. "Only sometimes he would tell me something was a law of God. I didn't know where he found out about them laws."

"Well, I guess it was church," he said. "I guess your papa just never happened to mention it." (Turned out, was what he was thinking; turned out of the church somehow on account of the woman that wore the blue silk spangledy dress, and then out of spite raised Mary Dove not to know there was such a thing as church.)

"What-all do they do at church?" she asked him.

"Well, like I said, they sing songs. People gets dressed up in their best clothes, and they go to the church house, and they sing and pray, and the preacher preaches to 'em about the laws of God."

"I wonder what kind of songs they sing," said Mary Dove.

"This is one I like," he said. He put the guitar down and sang in a high tenor voice a song strung out like a fine silk thread:

> *"I will arise and go to Jesus.*
> *He will embrace me in His arms.*
> *In the arms of my dear Savior,*
> *Oh there are ten thousand charms."*

The melody rose and fell. It sounded to Mary Dove a little like the songs she sang to God. She swayed with the music.

"Jesus?" she said.

"Surely your papa told you about Jesus. He's the son of God."

"Maybe he did," she said, "but I don't remember exactly. I never thought God was a man; I didn't know he would have a son."

"He ain't a man. Or not exactly. But his spirit come down and got into a woman and she had a son. And he was born on Christmas. Didn't you and your papa ever celebrate Christmas?"

"He told me about celebrating Christmas when he was a boy, but we never used to know what day it was. I didn't know it had anything to do with God."

"Well, it did. And the name of the mother of Jesus was Mary. Imagine you not knowing that."

"You oughtn't to be surprised by now," said Mary Dove, "at all the things I don't know."

"Seems like you'd know about Jesus anyway," he said.

"In the song," she said, "he sounds like a lover."

"I don't know about that," Red said doubtfully.

"What does it mean about the ten thousand charms?" Mary Dove asked him.

"Oh I don't know, Mary Dove," he said. "But someday I'll take you to church and you can hear preaching and learn all you want to know."

"I'd like to go and hear it all," said Mary Dove. "And I'd like to see the girls in their pretty dresses, and hear the people singing."

"You're supposed to go to worship God," Red said.

"Worship God?" she said. "I think I do that by myself, sometimes. Sometimes down in the pool, or up on the hill with the sky and clouds all around me, it seems like something gets in me and makes me feel–oh, I don't know, like I could nearly fly away. It seems like I'm knowing just how it is to be touched by God and feeling God in myself and knowing God is in everything. Did you ever feel that way, Red?"

"I don't know," he said. "Maybe a little."

"Do you think it's worshiping God?"

"It might be," he said. "I don't know very much about God."

"Papa said that. He said that very thing."

"Well, people don't," Red said. "Let's don't talk about that no more tonight–let's sing some more songs."

They couldn't get back into the spirit of singing, though, and at last Mary Dove took up the guitar and began to pluck from it thin music made out of sad and separate notes.

"I never heard the git-tar played like that," Red said.

She stopped. "I never had nobody to show me how to play," she said.

"Play on, Mary Dove," he said. "I never heard it played so pretty before, and that's the truth."

She played a little while, but when she thought he was asleep she put the guitar away. In a dark corner she changed to her shift and then went outside a little bit before she went to bed.

Right overhead she could see two stars. "The spell is over," she thought.

When she got back inside, Red had been up, doing what he had to do to get ready for bed. His britches were laid on the bench.

"How's the weather?" he asked.

"Clearing off," she said.

"Well, we need a change."

"Yes, we need a change."

"Good night," they said to each other.

But for a long time neither one slept. He lay tortured by an ache not caused by any wound, and when sometimes he dozed a little he seemed to be awakened by the singing of two lines:

"Who's gonna kiss your red-ruby lips
When I'm gone to a far-off land?"

The song about ten thousand charms went up and down, up and down, all through her, and she couldn't get out of her head the picture of Red (though she knew he wasn't the One) holding out his arms to her, offering her the ten thousand.

7

The next morning, Mary Dove said she thought she had better go and see about the cows again.

"I ought to go myself," said Red. "I nearly think I could."

"No, not yet," she said.

"Ride Sissy, then," he said to her. "Or Sangaree, if you want to."

"I'll walk," she said. "I'm used to walking, and I guess I can be gone all day if I need to."

"Yes, that might be good," he said. "Take something to eat."

"I am," she said. "And there's cornbread and a piece of meat for you."

When she started out, the lambs came running too. "Well howdy," she said to them. "I reckon you can come along, for it's a pretty day."

The clouds that had started breaking up in the night, now fiercely driven by the west wind, left behind wide spaces of pure blue, to be covered and uncovered, over and over again, as the wind swept earth and sky.

Mary Dove leaned into the wind, inviting the force of it, wanting it full in her face, needing something swept out of her.

The lambs would run with her, then turn sideways against the wind and run away a little, then turn and hurry back again. "You sillies," she said. Though she had seen them daily, she felt somehow as if she had been away from them a long time.

It seemed a long time since she had seen the blue sky. As she walked along the creek she felt glad the wind was blowing the fall leaves away; even the trees, she almost believed, were glad to have their branches free, bare against the sky.

She would like to be freed that way, she thought, of notions still lingering from the talk with Red last night. Her head was too full of all the different things he had told her, her heart (wasn't it what the songs called heart?) too full of Red. She scolded herself: did she think he had come as a sweetheart? He was there because she shot him in the leg.

She began climbing up the hill that rose sharply from the creekside, letting her skirt catch on bushes, not noticing what a steep and rocky way she unnecessarily took. Maybe the wind would blow the silliness out of her. That was what she said to herself. She didn't know whether she even hoped for anything more.

She came up on top of the hill against the sky, blowing–it seemed–with the clouds. Her skirt whipped around her. And then here came the lambs, left behind, baaing about it. Butting against her, one got halfway wrapped up in her skirt.

"You silly thing," she said, meaning it, wanting to be left alone. She bent to push at it, trying to straighten her skirt. There was a great tear in it, from a thorny bush she guessed, and the lamb had got its face half through the hole.

Oh, she thought, what will Red say?

Then she thought why should he say anything, it's not his dress. But she couldn't keep from thinking how glad he had been when they found the dresses, how pretty he said she looked in this dark red one.

I believe I can fix it, she thought. And that was all she was thinking about–fixing that dress. She had lost any chance of finding what she came to the hilltop for.

She went on, scolding the lambs, but she was not sure whether it was their fault or not.

Red, at the dugout, was restless and wondering too. He thought Mary Dove had gone off on purpose, to get away from him, and he thought it was a good thing she had. He didn't believe she would have any way to guess what ailed him, or what (if anything) affected her, but sometimes she seemed to have ways of understanding things she never had heard of. Whatever her reason, he was glad she was gone. He thought it would give him a chance to get straightened out, and he didn't aim to get in the shape he was in any more.

Like Mary Dove, he needed to get out of the dugout. He decided to put on his boots and walk around. His leg hurt, getting down to them, but he could manage.

The fresh wind and the sunshine (though it was coming and going) felt good. He stood under the arbor a little bit, getting used to the feel of his leg. He saw Sangaree grazing near the spring and whistled to him. The pony came running, and Sissy–a little farther away–looked up and whinnied.

"We'll be getting back to camp pretty soon," he said to them.

He thought he had better move around and exercise his

leg. He wouldn't be able to ride yet, he could tell, but he needed to get away from there as soon as he could.

And leave Mary Dove alone?

This was a question that had been coming to him all night. Of course he couldn't. The things she told him about the way she had lived since her father died didn't bear thinking of.

He found a stick to lean on in Mary Dove's pitiful woodpile and walked down toward the spring. Sangaree came along with him, to see what would happen.

"You're as bad as Mary Dove's lambs," Red said to him.

Well, he couldn't go on living in the dugout with her. He could tell that. He might do a lot of sorry things, but there was one thing he wasn't aiming to do to Mary Dove. He thought about old Pardue and the pains he had gone to, trying to protect her. Red might wonder about the old man and all he had done, but still it would seem like a sneaky trick to bury him and then come tearing after his daughter.

That wasn't the thing though. Old Pardue wasn't really the reason. It was just Mary Dove herself: you couldn't do it to her.

He couldn't keep living in the dugout. He would just have to go back to his camp as soon as he was able, and then come and see about her every day or two. Or he might fix him a place a little closer. That would do for a while—but when he left here? When he got fired, or quit, or went somewhere else?

He would have to think about that. There would be time.

He had got his leg to hurting, forgetting to be careful. He went back to the arbor and sat down on the bench. The sun, now fully shining, was on him there, and he sat a long time, forgetting to eat the dinner Mary Dove had left for him.

He was there when she came home.

She came and sat beside him. "The cows are just about where they was," she said.

He looked at her and nodded. How could he tell her she oughtn't to sit there?

"I'm glad you got out in the sun," she said. "It'll be good for you."

"For you too, I guess," he said. "Although you look just as brown and healthy as the first day I saw you."

"I never am out of the sun very long," she said.

"You're a regular sunflower," he said.

"I don't think I've ever seen a sunflower," she said.

"They say it faces the sun all day, from sunup to sundown."

"If I'as a flower, then," she said, "I think I'd like to be one."

He looked at her face all full of that notion, her eyes sparkling and her lips just a little apart.

"Then I would have to be your sun," he said.

"Yes, you could be my sun," she said.

He moved his face close to hers, and she moved to meet him. He knew the time had come when he must kiss her lips without holding back, and she would willingly let him.

When they quit kissing he said to her, "Mary Dove, we have got to get married."

(And what good had all his thinking done him, after all?)

"All right," she said.

He kissed her again on the lips, but lightly, quickly.

"And Red, do you know something?" she said then. "There didn't nobody ever tell me, but I think I know what getting married means."

Then he took her in his arms, and held her hard against him, and kissed her a long time again.

8

"That's enough of that," Red said in a little while.

"Is it, Red?" asked Mary Dove.

"Enough for now," he said. "Now you can start finding out what it's gonna be like to be my wife. I want you to go and cook me some dinner, for I forgot to eat the stuff you left for me. When a woman gets married she has to do what her man tells her to."

"Is that a law of God, like doing what your papa says?"

"I reckon it's a law of God," he said. "When we get married the preacher'll make you promise to obey me."

"I'll be glad to do what you tell me to," she said.

"Well, be off then," he said. "I'm gonna walk around a little while. You got me kind of messed up, you know."

"I know," she said.

Later when they were back in the dugout, eating the meal she prepared, she said to him, "Red, I wish you'd tell me some more about how folks gets married, and how they do after they get to be man and wife."

"Well, how we'll get married is we'll go to town some time and find a preacher to marry us, and probably we'll go to his house and we'll stand up together in front of him and promise to love each other always, and me take care of you, and you do what I say do, and then we'll be married and can live together all the rest of our lives and that will be all right."

"Couldn't we live together if we didn't get married?"

"It would be against the law."

"The law of God?"

"Yes," he said.

"What will we do when we're living together married?"

"Well, we'll just do kind of like we do now. Only I'll do my work and you'll stay around the house doing yours, and at night we'll sleep together."

"In the same bed?"

"Yes."

"Why will we do that?"

"'Cause that's how married folks does."

"Is that when they mate?"

He felt hot color coming into his face; he wished he could ever learn to tell what she was going to know and what she wasn't.

"Well, is it, Red? They do mate, don't they, because I know they have babies."

"Yes," he said, looking down at his plate. "I reckon that's when most folks does it."

"Do you think it feels good, Red?" she asked. "As good as kissing?"

"It's better," he said.

"You sound like you've done it, Red. Was you ever married?"

"No," he said shortly. "I ain't never been married, and I done it. Sometimes menfolks does, even if it is wrong, because they need it worse."

"Why do they, Red?"

"Now I ain't gonna talk no more about it," he said. "You'll find out when we get married, and that's soon enough."

He sounded like her father talking, telling her she didn't need to know. She wondered if there ever would be a way to find out all she wanted to know about things.

"Red," she said after a little silence. "I want to ask you something–not about getting married exactly. Can I?"

"I reckon," he said.

"Is there things that people just ain't supposed to talk about?"

"There's some things," he said.

"But if I ever do live where there's people, how will I know what I'm not supposed to say?"

"Well, you'll find out," he said. "You'll just find out. Some things is private. What a man and his wife does together in bed is one of them."

"Can they talk about it when they get married?" she asked.

"Oh Lord," he said. "I reckon, but I don't know any reason why they'd need to."

"Red, are you gonna get mad at me for wanting to know things?"

She was looking at him with the expression on her face that he called pitiful. It always made him feel so bad. "No, I ain't gonna get mad at you," he said, trying to be patient. "I know you got to have some way to find out."

"Then tell me something else," she said. "Papa never did talk much about God, and didn't tell me about Jesus, and all like you'as telling last night. And seemed like you didn't want to say much either. Ain't people supposed to talk about God and Jesus either? Is that another one of the things?"

"Oh Mary Dove, what a lot I got to teach you." He sighed. "Well, it ain't the same kind of thing, exactly, but most folks'd probably tell you it's a kind of a private thing. Most folks thinks going to church and hearing about it there is plenty. Then they just try to live all week like the preacher tells 'em, and they don't see no use in talking about it."

"Well," she said, "maybe I'll get to go to church some time, and then I'll find out everything."

"Yes," he said.

"Do you think we might live where there's a church some time?"

"I think we might," he said. "Or folks might start moving into this country and they'd build one right here."

"Right here at the dugout?"

"Well, right close. You never can tell. Would you like to keep on living here?"

"I've thought about that a lot, and I can't imagine living nowhere else. But then I thought it would be kind of good to live in a town, and see lots of folks, and go to church, and buy things when I need to."

"A town may come to us someday. It wouldn't surprise me, if we stayed here. I've thought about that, too, and I like this country so much–maybe I could get a chance to buy this land and we could stay here and build us a house some day right where the dugout is."

"With ten rooms and a front porch?"

"Maybe so," he said.

"Wouldn't that be fine?" she said.

"I think it would," he said. "But we've got a lot of time to decide, 'cause I'll have to work awhile for somebody else and get some money before I can strike out on my own."

"If we're married," she said, "I don't think anything else will make much difference to me."

"You'll be a good wife, Mary Dove," he said.

"Can I tell you what to do sometimes?" she asked.

"I reckon," he said.

"Then go lay down awhile," she said, " 'cause I think you've got too tired. And I'll take my dirty dishes to the spring and wash 'em."

"Well, but you'll have to do something for me first," he said.

"What, Red?"

"Come and kiss me."

She obeyed him.

Ah, she would be a good wife. She would have a lot of things to learn, of course, but he had never dreamed of a better wife than Mary Dove would be. Until he fell asleep, he was thinking more about the plan he had mentioned to her: homesteading the land where the dugout was, building a ranch around it, with a ten-room house full of boys to help him and pretty, gentle girls like Mary Dove to make it echo with laughing and singing.

When he woke up she had not come back and he wondered how late it was. He went out under the brush arbor to look for her, and it was later than he had thought but the sky was still light: clear as glass overhead and all across the west the color of Red's hair in full sunlight.

Mary Dove came and stood beside him. He took her hand and they stood together looking till the light faded, without having any need to say a word.

After supper he said to her, "The weather's so much better now, I believe I'll put my bed back out under the arbor and sleep there."

"Is it because you can't sleep good down here with me?" she asked him.

"What makes you say that?" he said.

"Oh I was thinking about the animals," she said. "I think that is the reason, and if it is I'll go sleep under the arbor. I like to do it anyway, when the weather's good enough, any time of the year. But the cool air might not be good for your leg."

"You're a funny girl, Mary Dove," he said. "Do you think I'm like a animal?"

"I guess we both are," she said. "Ain't we supposed to be?"

"Oh Mary Dove," he said.

"But we could both sleep down here," she said. "Looks like we could just go ahead and sleep together, since we've decided to get married."

"It ain't the same," he said.

"When will we get married?" she asked.

He hadn't really thought till then, only had been imagining that they would have to wait awhile, so he could get in good enough shape to support a wife. But what he said to her was "Just as soon as I get to where I can ride to town and back."

"Well then, if we're aiming to do it just as quick as we can, and the only reason we don't is on account of your leg, looks like it would be just the same if we went ahead."

"It ain't the same," he said.

"Tell me, Red," she said, "what does it do, standing up in front of the preacher and saying marrying words?"

"Well, I'll tell you, Mary Dove, what I heard a preacher say one time: after a man and a woman has been through a wedding ceremony it makes them just the same in their married life as Adam and Eve was in the Garden of Eden."

She looked up at him, her lips just parted.

"No, don't say it, Mary Dove," he told her. "I reckon you never have heard of Adam and Eve."

"Tell me about Adam and Eve, Red," she said.

"They was the first man and woman," he said. "God made them first, and all the rest of the people in the world from then on come from them. And when He made 'em he put 'em in this real pretty place where everything was just right. They had everything they wanted and as long as they obeyed God they never would have any trouble or sickness. They never would even die, but just live forever in the Garden of Eden."

"What happened, Red?" she asked, breathless, as he paused.

"Well, there was just one thing God told 'em they mustn't ever do. That was eat a apple from one particular tree in the garden. But the devil come, in the shape of a snake, and he talked Eve into taking a bite. And then she got Adam to eat some, too, because she was scared and wanted him to be with her in the punishment she knew they'as fixing to get. And sure enough, God did punish both of 'em, the way he said he would, and they had to leave the Garden of Eden and live lives full of trouble till at last they had to die."

Sitting close to Mary Dove in the firelight, he could see there were tears in her eyes.

"Oh Red," she said, "was it all the woman's fault?"

"In a way it was," he said. "He done it because he loved her. She was the first one to disobey God."

"She must have felt so bad about it," Mary Dove moaned. "Why couldn't she have done like God said?"

"Maybe the same reason you disobeyed your papa, and let me come into the dugout."

"Oh no," she said. "It wasn't the same reason a-tall. I couldn't of done nothing else, after I shot you."

Later, as she had said she would do, she took her bed out under the arbor. He told her it was all right, he wouldn't have any trouble sleeping, really, but she said she'd rather be where she could look at the stars anyway.

But after he thought she must be asleep, she came part of the way down the steps and called to him softly, "Are you asleep, Red?"

He wasn't, he told her.

"Could I ask you just one thing then?"
"All right."
"Red, what is the devil?"
"He's just the opposite of God," Red said, "and I ain't gonna try to tell you any more than that tonight."

9

He got so he looked forward to the questions she would ask, wondering what she would think of next. Sometimes he wanted to laugh at her about the things she didn't know, but that pitiful way of hers that touched his heart so deep kept him from laughter. Someday, he thought, when they were an old married couple sitting in rocking chairs on that front porch she wanted, he would remind her of this time and they would laugh together.

There was no end to the things she wanted to know about his sisters.

"Will they all get married some time?"

"They shore will if they can. Ain't no girl wants to be a old maid."

"Old maid?"

"That's what they call a woman that don't never get married."

"What does a woman do if she don't get married?"

"Well, if any of my sisters don't marry I reckon they'll go and live with one of the others, look after the children, and help around the place. There wouldn't one of 'em let another'n live in need of anything. They'd look after each other."

"When we get married won't I be kind of like their sister too?"

"Yes, you'll be their sister. A sister-in-law is what it's called."

"And will they love me too, and would they take care of me if I was in need?"

"Of course they'll love you!"

He knew they would, too, because nobody that knew Mary Dove could keep from loving her. But they wouldn't know what to think about some of the ways she did and some of the things she said. He would wait awhile, till she got a little more used to civilization, to take her home to his sisters.

Another time Mary Dove asked, "Where will the men come from, that the sisters will marry?"

"Why they're there all the time, living all around. I told you my folks live in a little old town–the girls goes to school with the boys, and to church with 'em, and couldn't get away from 'em if they wanted to."

"I just never can get in my head how a town really is," Mary Dove said. "But I guess what I was really wondering was how they find each other–how they decide which two will get married."

"They go a-courting. After a while a boy and girl gets to looking at each other, letting each other know they each think the other is the one they want to marry. You don't think that way about just everybody, you know. I knowed lots of girls, everywhere I been, but I never took to one the way I done you."

"Yes," she said. "I can't imagine how there could be any man but you that I would want to marry, but I wonder why that is."

"I don't know that. It's just the way things goes. But anyway, when a couple gets to thinking that way, they go places together, kind of pair off to get better acquainted, and then if they like each other as much as they thought they would, pretty soon they get married."

"Where do they go, a-courting?"

"Oh, lots of places. They might go to church together, Sunday morning. Then somebody might have a party–"

"A party?"

"That's where a bunch gets together at somebody's house and just has a good time. They have something good to eat and they play games. Like they all ring up in a circle and sing songs—this is a ring game I'm talking about. When they sing different parts of the song the circle breaks up and the couple holds hands and maybe goes to the center of the ring, or walks around it, or something like that, depending on what verse of the song they've come to."

"I guess I see. Is this when the girls wear their prettiest dresses?"

"They shore do, and they let their hair hang down in curls and maybe put ribbons in it. They like to show off, times like that, especially if they're courting."

"I wish I could go to a party some time."

"You'll get to."

When she talked that way he would get to feeling so sorry for her, thinking about all she had missed and all she didn't know or understand, that he would wish he could bundle her up right then and take her back home with him and make everything up to her. He would get mad at old Pardue, thinking of what he had done to Mary Dove—he must have been crazy, some way; that was all Red could figure.

There wouldn't be any quick way to make things up to her, though. He knew that. Too much time had been lost already. He began to feel impatient about the marriage. He didn't want to wait much longer to take her to town.

One day he got up with the determined notion of riding to look at the cattle he was hired to take care of. He ought to do that, at least. Besides, he would find out that way how able to ride he was—whether he thought he could get to town and back.

He didn't tell Mary Dove all his reasons, just said he had better go see about the cows.

"I hope it won't hurt you," she said.

"I don't think it will," he said.

He kissed her goodbye.

Just when he rode out of sight she knew she had never been so lonesome before. Maybe it was because she had learned that a man might not always come back, or maybe it was the difference between the ways a girl would feel about her papa and the man she was going to marry. She didn't know what the reason was, but she believed that if Red ever went away and failed to come back to her, she would surely die of lonesomeness.

That was a bright, clear day, with scarcely more than a breath of cool breeze blowing. As soon as Red left, Mary Dove went to work to clean out the dugout–she thought she would leave the door open all day to air the place, and carry all the bedding out into the sunshine to get rid of the dank dugout smell. With Red gone, she felt she couldn't bear any more of that damp, dark, closed-in feeling than she had to. She wanted to be breathing freely under the sunny sky.

Yet when she had finished her work she could think of nothing better to do than sit disconsolately under the brush arbor and look out across the hills.

By the place of the sun in the sky, by the length of the shadows on the grass, by the recollection of her own trips to look at the cows and the considered possibility of their having moved some miles farther away, Mary Dove tried to guess when he would come and where she would first catch sight of him.

She had never sat watching for her father this way. That thought came to her, and she wondered. Yes, she must truly love Red, and with the kind of love in the songs she had learned to sing so long ago, the kind of love that made parting between sweethearts the saddest thing there was to sing about. She must, in fact, be like other girls: like the girls that went a-courting, dressed in their finest clothes, to play in a singing, happy ring, hand in hand with the boys they loved.

If she were one of those girls, she would not be living always with the man she was going to marry. They would be in separate houses, and she would wait, this way, for him to come. What would she be doing? If they were going to a party, to play the singing games, she guessed she might spend a long time putting on her dress, making it look just right, combing and placing her hair, while she thought about the time that they would be together.

So thinking, she came upon a way to make the waiting easier and at the same time prepare a pleasant surprise for Red. He would be tickled to come home and find her dressed up the way she would be if she had really been a girl in the town where he used to live and he had come a-courting her.

She went and took the silver-spangled dress out of the trunk. Like everything else in the dugout, it smelled of damp earth, and she carried it out into the sunshine and shook it in the breeze. She didn't believe any girl in Red's town could have a prettier dress than this.

She hung it, as she hung things to dry, over a low, thornless bush. While it aired she took rags and went to wash herself at the spring. She did not consider, that cool fall day, a bath in the big pool down the creek, but presently moved on down and took her comb from its place in a big cottonwood and sat on a rock while she took her hair down and combed it. There was a comb she could use at the dugout, but she rarely remembered it: her pleasure was to come where she could sit by the pool and let the breeze lift her hair. What Red exactly meant by the girls letting their hair hang down in curls she did not know; but she knew her own hair was curly (so her father had called it, comparing it with his own straight light-colored hair), and she thought if she combed it loose she might at least look more like a girl going to a party than ordinarily she did.

Back at the dugout she found a wide blue ribbon (she had always called it sky blue) just about the color of the dress, and she bound her hair back out of her face with it. She could just glimpse it in the steel mirror hanging by the dugout door.

"Next time I go to town I'll bring you a real looking glass," her father had said. "A gal as pretty as you are needs to know it."

"Am I really a pretty gal, Papa?"

"The prettiest. Prettier than your mama, even."

She couldn't tell much about what she looked like, peering into that shadowy steel glass. She did like the way the ribbon held her hair back, though.

Outdoors, not seeing any sign of Red coming, she pulled off her calico dress and slipped the shiny blue one down over her. She hadn't realized it had no sleeves. At first she couldn't tell how it was supposed to go, but then she got it arranged with the part like a ruffled collar barely covering her shoulders and coming down so low in front that, if it hadn't been easy to tell where the waist ought to be, she would have thought she had it on wrong. She had thought breasts were always covered up, but all the top half of hers showed above the tight spangled waist of this dress. The skirt was about as short as the shifts she had worn in the summer. She did not like the way her homemade shoes looked below the soft full skirt, and decided no shoes at all would be better.

Looking down at the dress, she wondered if there could be anything people might buy at a store any prettier than it was. As nearly as could be possible, she thought, it looked like the sky after the spring blizzard, when trees lifted spangles of glittering ice against the deep blue.

For the first time in her life she really longed for a looking glass, and she decided to go and look at her reflection in the pool. It was disappointingly dark. No color showed, because the sun was already too far down the sky. But she liked the shape of herself in the dress with the full blowing skirt and her hair like a fresh-blown-up cloud.

Suddenly it seemed to her that she had taken a long time getting ready for the imagined party. Red might come to the dugout and find her gone–this would ruin the surprise. She must hurry. She began running along the creek, her hair and skirt flying, the lambs–that she had paid no mind to–following not far behind.

As she came up out of the creek by the dugout, she

noticed that Red was just coming over the hill from the opposite direction. She stood on the grass in front of the brush arbor, panting a little, trembling with her sense of the joyful surprise he would have when he came near enough to see what she had done for him.

10

As soon as they saw her from the top of the rise, Sangaree began to move faster. If Red gave any sign of the surge of eagerness within him he wasn't aware of it, but somehow it made itself known to Sangaree.

Bushes came up cutting off the sight of her, and then when he moved out of the creek, where the trail led him, she had come down toward the spring and he was almost upon her, nothing between them in the clearing. He had to pull up hard on the reins to keep from running over her.

Her. Oh it was Mary Dove standing there. But before her name could sound itself in his brain it was lost. Lost and drowned beneath a rushing, deafening roar that pounded through him like long-drawn-out thunder.

"Nigger!"

There in the yellow light with her hair like a mass of fine glinting wire and her breasts shining brown as her sun-loving face she stood revealed to him.

Seeing his face, Mary Dove forgot all she had done to surprise him and moved to reach for his hand. "Oh you hurt yourself," she said. "The wound wasn't well after all."

Her voice came clear above the deafening roar within him, stilled the beating in his brain a little. Mary Dove was still there, still somehow there, and whatever destroying power had fallen upon them he must save her if he could. Whatever he had to do now, Mary Dove (his love) must be saved and protected.

"I'm all right," he said. "I got tired, and I want to go and wash my face at the spring."

"I'll take your horse," she said, and led him quietly away as Red went slowly to the spring.

The splash of cold water cleared some of the confusion of his mind. He rose and turned toward her as she came shyly smiling back to him.

"I'as playing like you would come a-courting," she said, "and I dressed myself up for a party."

He sadly smiled, and bent and kissed her on her dark (not sunbrowned) forehead.

"You are the prettiest thing in the world, Mary Dove," he said to her.

"Am I really, Red?" she asked.

She was two things. Mary Dove, and this new thing that threatened, against which some action must be taken, some battle pitched. Confusion was rising again within him, and he knew escape was the only thing that could save him—save him and her. There would be something to do, he could think of something, if only he could get away from her awhile.

"You are so pretty, Mary Dove," he said, "that I can't hardly stand to think about what I got to do. But the cows are in kind of a mess over yonder, and I got to go back and straighten things out."

She looked quickly down. Tears slipped along her cheek.

"I got to go back to my old camp and stay awhile, close to the herd. I'll get fired if I don't look after it, you know."

"I know, Red," she said. "I'll gather up some things for you to take back with you."

"Listen, I'll leave Sissy with you," he said, "and you can come to me if you need help."

"I'll be all right," she said.

He was following her into the dugout. She was getting together his clothes, his blankets, a few things to eat.

"Listen, Mary Dove, I'll be back. I wouldn't do this if I didn't have to." God knew that was the truth.

"Will you eat some supper before you go?" she asked. That was also her answer.

"No, I'd better go on," he said.

"Well then."

They went back out into the sunlight. (How could he ever have failed to see what color she truly was?) She stood near him while he tied his bedroll on behind the saddle.

"Kiss me goodbye again, Red," she said at last.

He put down the threatening darkness within. (Oh God, oh Mary Dove.) He turned and embraced her, crushingly kissed her, trying to press out the ache that now possessed him.

"What is it, Red?" she asked when at last he let her go.

"Just goodbye for a few days, Mary Dove."

That was all he could say. He quickly turned away, hurried to mount Sangaree and ride away from her, for he needed the relief of flowing tears. He trusted Sangaree to know where they were going. He couldn't see the trail.

He could hear her calling "Goodbye, sweetheart," but didn't dare to turn around and face her. Her dressed up for him in that cheap dance-hall dress, and the tears now gushing (he knew as though he had turned to look) down her cheeks, and down and on down, splashing on her beautiful brown breasts.

11

She never did doubt him. That was what he believed, wished he didn't have to believe, but came back to as regularly as he rode the wide circle of useless miles around the cattle herd every day. Guessing no reason for a lie, she would wait, wondering what terrible thing had happened to the cows, how long it would take him to do whatever had to be done and come back home to her. Sad and lonely she would wait–how long, before she feared he never would return?

Even then she might never doubt, but only grieve for him, wandering over the hills and valleys looking for his remains as she had looked for her father's. He never did take her to see that grave. Never had. At least he ought to keep that promise.

Because of course he must go back. Whatever she was, he couldn't abandon her. It would be kinder to shoot her, as he had shot the motherless calves after the blizzard. He could imagine the life he would have, the question of just what day or year she starved to death never answered.

Whatever she was, he had made himself responsible for her. Of course he had been a fool, had been blind, not to see from the start. But there she was, living her days out under the summer sun, with never a bonnet on her head or shoes and stockings on her feet. He had known many a white girl with eyes and hair as dark as hers, and who would have questioned that golden brown skin? Anybody but a fool, was probably the answer to that. Anybody might have noticed that her skirt never slipped high enough to show any white leg; anybody might have recognized her smiling wide mouth for what it was.

Part of the time, riding his rounds, he could excuse himself. The first time he saw her close, he was out of his head; even when he came to and talked to her, there under the arbor, he was hurting so he guessed he wasn't at himself. Then, all through the time he was getting to know her, falling (fool that he was) in love with her, they were down in the dugout where there was scarcely enough light to tell black from white even in the daytime.

It really must be true that love is blind, he often told himself. By the time they came up into the light, it was too late. She had well deceived him.

Only such a shock as he got the day he found her waiting for him with breasts bare and hair unbound could have restored his sight. Why did she thus shamelessly undeceive him?

Shameless deceiver. Sometimes he said those words aloud, fiercely. Why had she deceived him, why undeceived? It could have been no trick to marry him, for then she would have waited longer to reveal the truth.

Sometimes he wished it had been such a trick unmasked. He would have known what to think about that. (Back home, a trial that had the whole town trying to squeeze into the courthouse, and he was just a boy but still remembered the things the young men told: "They made her strip to the waist, right before the judge and jury and everybody–only the women had to leave the courtroom. And anybody could see what she was, but the feller claimed he didn't know it till he married her. He didn't get by with that though.")

Oh, he would have known how to be angry if the trick had been that, if she had been trying to make him break the law so she could be a white man's wife, live white.

Because she could probably pass for white, for a little while. Folks would guess and gossip, and the truth would get to be known, but she could brazen it out awhile if that was what she wanted to do.

He couldn't tell how much Negro blood she might have, but that would make no difference to the law. Her mother probably wasn't full-blooded, herself. Red wondered if she could have been white enough to trick old Pardue. Probably not, he thought; probably they never went through a marriage ceremony, but it wouldn't make any difference if they did because it still wouldn't be legal. Mary Dove was still a bastard. A part-nigger bastard.

And that explained everything. At least it explained a lot. Why Pardue left her alone when he went to town, why he taught her to shoot any man that came near her, let her grow up ignorant of so many things. He might have been crazy enough to believe he could keep her from ever finding out what she was.

A part-nigger bastard. Could you be part nigger and not know it, not feel it somehow? And if you could, if you didn't know, wasn't it somehow the same as not being at all?

When he came around to that, Red would put spurs to Sangaree. And that was a thing he had never done. "It's done drove me crazy," he thought. He would go like the wind, never looking where he rode, never caring.

He couldn't get away from that crazy thing about himself, though, from the crazy notion he had let into his mind. Even if Mary Dove didn't know (and she didn't know, she couldn't have guessed), did he think this would change the law somehow? The law that would punish by imprisonment a man who did what Red intended, God's law that would send him to hell?

And the answer to that was that if she didn't know, he did. And he would have to go back and tell her, for she waited (he came full circle again) at her dugout trusting him and never doubting his return.

When he got straightened out in his mind a little better, he would have to go back: he had made her his responsibility, he had been blind and a fool, she was innocent and loved him. He made the full circle again.

Warm, sunny days passed–warm for December. He knew it must be December. He had a pocket calendar, on which he had meant to mark off the days, but he hadn't looked at it since the day he got shot. Now he thought back, tried to count and remember, and decided that it must be close to Christmas. At home his sisters would be going to the church house, putting up red and green rope. He hoped they had a turkey.

You had to celebrate Christmas some way. He decided he would go and see Mary Dove. He guessed his visit wouldn't be much of a present for either one of them, but it would surely be an occasion to remember. Christmas would mark and seal it.

12

Mary Dove never knew how many days had passed, but on every one of them she sat on the brush arbor bench and watched for him and wondered. He must have had to go far away from there, she began to believe. Sometimes she was tempted to go and look for him, but he had said to her, "Come if you need me," and she knew he hadn't meant the need of his kiss or his touch.

At night the cow bawled for her, the hens went in to roost, and the lambs (not really lambs any more, and crowding their pen) came home. These were her companions.

Often she took out her guitar on sunny afternoons and sang for many hours of lovers parted. This seemed to be what those songs had always been preparing her for—this waiting.

One day as she sat looking out for him he came. She saw him at the top of the rise, and walked to meet him while he came, out of sight, through the bushes.

She went putting her arms up to him, like a child, and he came down into them and kissed her as she expected to be kissed.

That was all he could have done. That was what he thought afterward, but at the time he didn't think. It seemed like something he had been doing all his life.

"Here," he said, "I brought you a present."

She looked into the bag he handed her and saw a mess of quails.

"What for this time?" she asked.

"Christmas," he said. "Leastways I'm calling it that, and I thought we ought to celebrate by having something good to eat for Christmas dinner."

"Is that what you do at home?" she asked. "What your sisters do?"

"Oh, they cook lots of stuff," he said.

"Then I will too. I have still got some sugar, and I'll make a patty cake."

"All right," he said. "You can fix it for dinner tomorrow. That'll be Christmas, if my figuring's right. Today is Christmas Eve."

"Do we celebrate Christmas Eve too?"

"We may," he said. "At least we can talk."

"Well, go put up your horse, and I'll dress the quails for tomorrow, and then we can talk. You can tell me what you've been doing."

When he came back he said, "I'm gonna build a fire while you finish that. I'd kind of like to sit by the fire."

She came in after dressing the quails and sat on the bench in front of the fire, looking to him to sit by her.

"I'm gonna set over here, Mary Dove," he said, pulling up the stool they had always used at the table. "I got to talk about some things I can say better if I ain't too close to you."

"All right," she said, and waited.

"Mary Dove, I lied to you," he said.

"You what?"

"I lied." He wondered how he was ever going to tell her anything. "You do know what lying is, don't you?"

"Yes," she said, "I know what lying is."

"The cows was all right all the time," he said. "I just had to get away from you."

"Away from me?" she asked, surprised.

"You'll understand why, in a little bit," he said. "First I just got to ask you one thing, and I want you to tell me. You don't remember your mother a-tall, do you? Not anything about the way she looked, or whether she was dark or light?"

"Not anything, Red."

"All right, then. I think I've got a idea what she looked like. I expect she looked a lot like you, only darker. Your papa was a white man, I know that, but Mary Dove, I nearly know your mama was a nigger."

He paused. She didn't say anything.

"Don't you see what that means?" he demanded.

"You told me one time," she said. "It's a pity to think of it, but she's dead now, and maybe it don't matter, where she's gone to."

"I hope it don't," he said, "but the thing you don't seem to understand is that if she was you are too."

"How could that be? Like you said, Papa was a white man."

"That don't matter," he said. "By the law, if you've got any nigger blood in you a-tall, that makes you a nigger."

"What law?"

"Well, just the law. State law, I reckon."

"Not God's law?"

"No–oh, I don't know. God's law too I guess. I just know it makes you a nigger."

"Does it mean you can't love me? Is that against the law?"

"Yes. Well, anyway, marrying is. We can't get married, Mary Dove, and that's the thing you got to know."

"I wanted us to marry."

"I did too, more than anything I ever wanted before. But we can't, that's all."

"How come you to find out my mama was a nigger?" she asked after a little time when neither spoke.

"I'm guessing about your mama," he said, "because of what I found out about the way you look. That day you put on the blue dress–and it come down so low."

"I wondered about that," she said. "I hadn't ever thought women wore clothes that showed so much of theirselves."

"They don't, mostly," he said. "I reckon your mother was some kind of dancer–or something. The thing is, I thought your skin was tanned from the sun, but it's that color all over, year around, ain't it?"

"I'm dark all over," Mary Dove said. "Darker than Papa was, darker than you."

"And your hair–it's nigger hair: not as kinky as some, but nigger hair for sure. I never noticed that, till you combed it out that day. You ain't like a full-blooded nigger, Mary Dove, and you're a awful pretty girl. But the law's the law."

"And the law says we can't get married."

"It does. There ain't no way we could, no way a-tall. But I'll look after you somehow. I'll see you're took care of, I'll figure out a way."

"I'll figure out a way," she repeated dreamily. "That's what Papa used to say."

"I see now why he done the things he did," Red said. "Why he kept you away from folks."

"He never did figure out anything," she said, "and I don't reckon you ever will either. On account of that law. That silly law. Red, it don't make no sense. How come they got such a law?"

"It makes sense. White folks and niggers just ain't supposed to mix."

"To mate, you mean?"

"I reckon I do."

"Well, it just don't make no sense, that's all. How can the law say folks ain't supposed to mate?"

"Well–there's your law of God, Mary Dove. It's a law of God, is what it is."

"How do you know?" she asked. "Does the preachers say so in the church house?"

"Of course they do–they must. I can't remember whether I ever heard one say it or not, but I know they do. Everybody knows that."

"Where can the preachers find out about laws of God?"

"From a book. The Bible."

"Have you read it?"

"Not much. I ain't much at reading, and besides, that's what preachers is for–to tell you what it says."

"I don't believe it's in that book. I always believed everything Papa ever told me about the laws of God, and up to now I believed everything you told me, but I just don't believe it because it don't make no sense. I can see why sheep and cows ain't supposed to mate: now, that's a law of God; if creatures ain't supposed to mate then they're fixed so they can't. And I reckon if what you say is so then niggers and white folks ain't fixed that way–because here I am, and I don't know what you can say to that."

"You just don't understand."

"I understand you want me to believe something you can't even remember hearing a preacher say and something that might be in a book but you don't know because you never did read it." Sudden fire flashed in her eyes–a burning he'd never expected.

"I know it's against the law of the state, anyway," he said. "There was a man from my own town sent to prison for breaking it. I'm really not lying to you, Mary Dove."

She jumped up. "Oh Red," she cried, "I never thought you was. I just don't see how I can bear it, that's all."

She ran up the steps, out of the dugout, weeping and moaning (it seemed to Red) like a mourner at a funeral. He went after her, calling "Mary Dove, Mary Dove!"

She was running down toward the creek. "Stop, Mary Dove!" he cried. "I can't run good enough to catch you–don't do me this away."

She stopped and looked back at him. "Come back," he begged.

She turned and walked slowly toward him. She was sobbing, but quietly now. "There can't be a law to make me not love you, Red," she said. "Seems like there's some kind of a law in me that says I got to, and says when you call me I got to come."

He knew she was right. He had that law in him, too. He let her come against his chest, and held her while they wept together.

"Oh God, oh God," he said.

"Are you calling God to come?" she asked.

"I'm praying, I reckon," he said.

She still leaned against him. "Tell me the truth, Red," she said to him, "do you believe it's a law of God that says we mustn't marry?"

"I don't know," he said. "I have always believed it–I still believe it must be in the Bible somewhere, but it's hard to figure out how God could want to keep us apart."

"I don't think God does, Red," she said. "I don't think that state law has anything to do with God a-tall."

"It might be so, Mary Dove," he said. "I just don't know."

"If we could be married by God's law, Red, would you care about the state?"

"The state wouldn't call it marriage."

"I wouldn't care. Would you?"

"You don't know what you're saying, Mary Dove. If we wasn't married by the law, we never could live like ordinary people. We couldn't go to church together. Our children wouldn't even have a name. I couldn't take you home to see my sisters–they would think you was a shameful woman and keep you out of the house."

"Would it be that way?" she said.

"Yes it would, Mary Dove."

"Even if we told them we married by God's law?"

"Even then."

She waited a little while, then sadly said, "Then I'll be sorry, but we'll do it anyway."

"Do what?"

"We'll marry."

"How can we do that?"

"Do you remember one time I told you ways I find God?"

"I remember what you told me," he said. "But how can you know it's God?"

"It just is God. There has to be some way to get to God, for folks that don't know about churches and preachers. Maybe if they got churches they don't never find out about this way, because they don't need to."

"I never thought of that," he said.

"We can go and find God now," she said, "and stand right before God instead of a preacher, and promise each other all the things we're supposed to promise. And then we will be married, and God will know, and the rest won't make no difference."

"I don't know," he said.

"We'll be just like Adam and Eve in the garden."

"The woman tempted me," he muttered.

"What?" she asked.

"Nothing," he said. "We will do it, Mary Dove." They would do it because he must have her or die, and because this way she could feel like his wife and he would have a chance to make her happy. In the end, of course, they would go to hell.

13

"Do you like my red dress best?" she asked him after a little while, when they were seated under the arbor.

"I believe I do," he said.

"Then I will go and put it on," she said, "and it will be my wedding dress."

"Are we going to do it now?" he asked.

"What would we wait for?" she answered.

"We won't wait," he said. "Only, since you're fixing to dress up I believe I'll take a bath and shave."

By the time they were ready to climb the hill behind the dugout to the place Mary Dove had chosen for their wedding, the sun was about to go down.

"Can you climb the hill? Is your leg good enough?" she asked him anxiously.

"It's fine," he said. "We'll go wherever you say."

She took his hand and led him up a narrow trail made long before by her father's sheep. As they ascended they heard some noise behind them and looking around, beheld the remnant of those old herds: the spring lambs coming.

"Oh, I ought to have shut up them sheep," said Mary Dove.

"Let 'em alone," he said. "There needs to be guests at a wedding."

"If they'll behave," she said.

The sheep followed quietly at a little distance, keeping back perhaps because the man was there.

At last Mary Dove and Red stood together hand in hand on the hilltop. No trees or bushes grew there, and scarcely any grass; the ground was thickly strewn (as from some great careless hand) with pebbles turned yellow-gold by the sinking sun.

There was no higher hill close around them. Below them spread a land of purple shadows, and all around them was the pale green sky, alive with wing-shaped clouds of blazing gold, moving toward the sun.

"I don't think I ever saw the sky like this," Red said in a low voice.

"I have," Mary Dove said. "I used to play like the clouds was birds that belonged to sundown, flying home to roost."

"What are they really?"

"Wings of God," she said. "Do you feel it?"

He shivered. "I think I do," he said.

Close to the sun the clouds turned fiery red. The sun disappeared among them.

"I have always been by myself before," she whispered. "Will it come for two?"

"It will for me and you," he said, "for now I know I've been close to it before."

"It is God," she said.

"I don't know what else it could be," he said.

They stood waiting. The sheep off away from there a little at the brow of the hill stood waiting, too, turned toward sunset.

The fire died down. Cloud colors softened.

"Have we missed it?" he whispered.

"No. Wait," she answered. "Sometimes I sing."

"Sing," he said.

There had been no song made for this time. She thought of one he had taught her, one they had sung together. In a whispery voice she sang of the ten thousand charms.

That music moved through him and joined him to the spread-out sky.

She hushed. Then "Look," she barely whispered, and stretched out her hand to the west.

A small cloud fragment hung there, thin as down, loosed

from some golden wing. It turned to palest pink but still was lit by the sun's fading gold. Within it a star shone, steady and clear.

"Ahhhh," she breathed.

"Is it time?" he asked.

"It is time," she said. "Let us promise."

They promised all the things that Red had ever told her of: that they would love and cherish each other, that she would obey him and he would take care of her, always and always.

Then he drew her to him and embraced and kissed her.

"Now we are man and wife," he said, "till death do us part."

Now the cloud was gone and the star shone alone in a clear sky.

"I hope it's the Christmas star," he said. "I hope it's a blessing."

Not knowing what he meant, still she knew it must be. "It's a blessing, Red," she said.

They turned and started down the hill. The sheep, seeing them coming, moved on ahead down the trail, leading them home.

III

Sisters

About a week after Mary Dove and Red got married, the long warm spell of weather ended and they had some snow. Mary Dove went outside first and discovered it. The ground was covered, and feathery flakes were thinly falling still.

"Come on out here!" she called to him.

As he came out under the arbor, she hit him in the chest with a snowball that sprayed all over him.

"You rascal!" he yelled, and started after her.

She slowed to let him catch her, not wanting him to be running on account of his bad leg. As he grabbed her they slipped and fell down together, laughing, into a drifted bank of snow.

Though she was faster, her strength was nothing against his. He pinned her arms down and rubbed her face with snow.

"You're freezing me," she complained.

"I'll kiss it warm," he said, and covered her face with kisses.

Her arms freed, she threw them both around his neck and held his face to hers, kissing him back.

"Let's go back in the dugout," he said.

"Let's do," she said.

They went back in to where they had made their two beds into one and cast themselves upon it, doing once again the thing that through the days and nights of their week together had brought them both delight.

("What do they call it, Red?" "I don't know of no name for it that a man can say to a decent woman.")

Mary Dove got up and put some wood on the fire. Then they lay awhile together, their hands just touching, watching the blaze.

At last Red said, "I can't lay around here all day. I got to go see about them cows—they may get restless in this snow."

"Soon as we get some breakfast," Mary Dove said, "I'll get ready and go with you."

"You ain't worried about me going off? This ain't no blizzard, you know."

"I ain't worried," she said. "I just want to go with you."

"Well, I don't see why not," he said. "I'll go milk while you see to things here."

"Milking's my job," she said.

"You've done mine a-plenty," he said.

"I'll help you today," she said. "We'll work together."

She put on the cut-off britches she wore for riding. Red said he would get her a side saddle some time—then he had to explain what that was, and they laughed together again about her ignorance.

They were almost in sight of the Badger Creek camp when they came to the herd, and Red decided to move it nearer his new headquarters, to a wide flat creek valley where grass grew so tall it showed above the snow. Mary Dove turned out to be a good helper.

"I've herded sheep all my life," she said in answer to his surprise. "Cows ain't too different."

"I never had a better partner," he said when the job was done.

After that she always went with him. Some days in the middle of winter would seem just like spring, and then they often stayed out on the hills together from daylight to dark.

One time she said to him, "Red, are we very far from where you buried Papa?"

"A mile or two," he said. "I'll take you there."

They rode first to the top of the hill that dropped off to form a bluff above the creek. Looking down, they could see white bones piled.

"You found Papa there," she said.

"Under that overhang."

"I still wonder how it could have happened."

"Well, he knew the country. I reckon his horse must've slipped. That might have happened if the sheep went over the bluff, and he was after 'em. I kind of thought they just drifted up the creek and piled up on each other, but I couldn't tell."

"Old Shep must've been under the sheep."

"I never seen no dog."

"Well, it can't matter now, how it happened. Let's go to the grave."

They went back down to a lower gentler hill and found the flat rock Red had moved there. There wasn't much sign of a grave, for grass had covered it.

They stood together looking down at it. Red took off his hat.

"There wasn't much I could see to do," he said.

"You done good, Red. I knowed he ought to be buried, but I don't see how I could have done it by myself."

Red took out his knife and squatted down. "I aimed to come back and carve his name," he said. "I think I will now."

She sat on the grass beside him. "I wish you would," she said.

They sat quietly a long time while he cut the letters big and deep. When he had finished she traced them with her finger. *PARDUE.*

"What does it mean, Red?" she asked.

"Mean?" he said.

"Seems like names means things," she said. "You told me why you was called Red, and I know about Christopher Columbus. And now you've told me about Mary, and of course I know about doves. But what is Pardue?"

"I reckon lots of names has got meaning," he said, "or had once. I've heard that was so, but folks has forgot most of the things they mean. I guess whatever meaning Pardue had is lost."

"It means my papa, anyway," she said. She went to Red and kissed him, and her tears wet both their faces. He held her and let her cry a little while.

Then they strolled together up to the greening hilltop and came to a slab of rock they both could sit on, so they sat (without saying why they would, or thinking of it) hand in hand looking out over the wide land.

Down in the hollow, a dove cooed.

"Spring's close," said Mary Dove.

The air seemed thick with spring. The sky was clear blue, but the air was moist and laden with odors of greening.

To the south, the country was what they called open. The hills were scattered and small; beyond them, the land rose flat against the horizon, even with the tops of the hills. Mary Dove had never been that far.

"What is on the high land, Red?" she asked him now.

"Not much," he said. "Grass, and not hardly any trees. It's what folks calls the Divide–between the Brazos and the Colorado rivers. On the other side, all the creeks runs into the Colorado. This side, it's the Brazos."

"Does the water from our creek get into the Brazos River at last?"

"It does."

"And where does the river go?"

"The Gulf of Mexico," he said. "And that don't go nowhere, because it's a ocean. Big ships sails on it, a-going to all the countries of the world."

"Have you been to the ocean, Red?"

"No, I never did see the ocean."

"I can't hardly think about how it must be. Can't you see the other side of it?"

"You could travel for weeks and still not see the other side."

"If I was to go down to the end of our creek, and on down the one it runs into, on to the Brazos River, and on and on to the ocean, and get on a ship–could I get to Africa?"

"Africa?"

"Ain't that where the niggers comes from?"

"That's what I told you, Mary Dove."

"Well, could I get there?"

"I reckon you could."

"And if I did–would they like me there? Could I marry a man there, and would his sisters take me in?"

"I reckon they would, I don't know. Ain't no sense in talking like that."

"I reckon they wouldn't. Because you know what, Red? I look like a nigger to you but I'd look like white folks to them. And they wouldn't want me neither."

He pulled away from her, stood up abruptly. "Don't never talk like that again," he said.

She got up and took his arm. "Oh, I never meant that, Red. Don't be mad at me, I know you want me. I just meant–white folks. But I ain't gonna think about them no more. And you ain't white–you're Red."

She tried to laugh; she wished he would. "I thought that was kind of funny," she said.

"It is, kind of," he said. "But I don't seem to feel like joking."

"We better go," she said.

"Yes," he said, but they kept standing there. Mary Dove guessed he felt the way she did and didn't want to start home till all the bad feeling had gone out of them. They had never known anything but good feeling in their dugout, and she hoped they never would.

They stood looking off to the southern horizon, and suddenly something rising into the sky above it caught her eye. At first she thought it was something she had never seen before.

"Look, Red," she said, pointing. "Look away over yonder. What is it?"

She knew the answer, though, before he spoke. "Smoke," he said shortly. "You can see smoke a long ways on a day like this."

"Somebody had to build the fire," she said.

"There might be somebody a-camping over there," he said. "It ain't got nothing to do with us though."

But still he pulled her fiercely against him, as though protecting her against some threat.

"Now listen to me, Mary Dove," he said. "I wasn't mad at you while ago–just mad at everything in general, I reckon, because I want so bad to give you everything you'd like to have and there ain't no way I can. I'd give anything in the world if I could bring you a dozen sisters for a present."

"I know you would, Red."

"You remember that verse I made up and sung to you?"

"I remember."

"Well, don't you forget it, because I meant it then and I mean it now. I aim to be papa and mama to you, and sisters and everything, just like I sung to you."

She hugged him. "Sing it to me now, Red," she teased. "Tell me who's gonna shoe my pretty little foot."

"I don't feel much like singing," he said.

She pulled away from him and went and sat down on the rock again, and took off both her shoes. "Now come on," she coaxed him. "Come and set down and sing to me, and I'll let you shoe my feet." She looked up at him laughing and stretched out her arms.

"You may have to offer me more than that," he said, "if I sing that silly song."

"Sing it then," she said.

He sat down beside her and sang:

"Red's gonna shoe your pretty little foot,
Red's gonna glove your hand,
Red's gonna kiss your red-ruby lips,
And Red's gonna be your man."

He turned and kissed her lips then, and they made love on top of the hill, out under the open sky.

2

"I can't get over how we do," said Red one rainy day.

They had got up that morning and done what work had to be done, and then gone back to bed and now, hours later, Mary Dove was up cooking breakfast and he still lay in bed.

"How do we do, Red?" Mary Dove asked.

"Not like any man and wife I ever heard tell of," Red said. "The man's supposed to be gone to work all day, and they don't never go to bed together till after supper when it's dark and they've blowed the lights out."

"Do you wish we done more like other folks?"

"Lord no," he said, "but sometimes I can't keep from imagining what a fit my sister would have if she was to come in on us a time like this."

"I guess different folks has different ways," said Mary Dove. "I reckon our way is all right."

"It suits me," said Red. "Course when we start having children we might have to do different."

"When will we, Red?" asked Mary Dove.

"Well, we can't tell about that," he said. "Just when the Lord sends 'em. Sometimes a couple will be married several years before a baby comes."

"Do you mean they can mate and they still might not start a baby?"

"That's right, they don't always."

"I hope we will, pretty soon," Mary Dove said.

"I'd just as soon we waited awhile, myself," Red said. "I'd

like to know for sure how we're gonna live, and have a little money ahead, before we start a family."

"I'd like to have a baby though," Mary Dove said.

"How do you know?" Red said. "You don't know nothing about it. It ain't so easy for women to have babies, Mary Dove. They're liable to suffer a lot, and they can't do no work for two or three weeks."

"Why is that so, Red?" Mary Dove asked. "Tell me, how does a woman do when she has a baby?"

"Oh Mary Dove, I don't know. A man don't watch a woman have a baby."

"Will I have to do it by myself?"

"No," he said roughly. "It ain't fixing to happen any time soon, and we'll figure out some way. Now let's have breakfast, and talk about something else."

Mary Dove guessed she had come upon another one of the things men and women weren't supposed to talk about, so she didn't ask Red any more about it. She didn't believe it could be much the way he thought it was, anyhow; it must be an easy and natural thing to have a baby.

"Well," she said as they sat down to eat. "It don't take the creatures I know about several years to get a baby. I bet we'll have new lambs before spring comes again."

"Sheep multiplies fast," he said.

"My silly little old lambs will be a herd of sheep before you know it," she said.

"If I don't watch," Red said, "I may get to be a sheep man before I know it."

"Would you think that was bad?"

"Oh I don't know. I thought I couldn't stand sheep, but now that I've been around some for a while I don't know as they're much worse than a bunch of crazy cows."

"Papa made a living for us, raising sheep."

"I know it," Red said. "I've been thinking about that. Seems like a man might get started faster raising sheep, and maybe not need as much land."

"Ain't the land free to anybody that wants to use it?" Mary Dove asked.

"It is now," Red said, "but it won't be very long. Folks'll be moving in, like we talked about, and they'll get pieces of land for their own, and nobody else won't be able to use it for anything."

"How do they get it?"

"They buy it. But sometimes the state lets 'em have it cheap, with a long time–maybe forty years–to pay all the money. I figure if I could get this land here, with the dugout already built, and a water supply handy, we wouldn't have much trouble paying for it at last."

"Could you get it, Red?"

"I don't know for sure. I'll be having to go to town one of these days, and I might get a chance to find out."

"How much could you get, do you reckon?"

"I've heard you can get four sections, the way I was talking about, from the state. I can't tell you just exactly how much that would be, but if this place was in the middle of it, it would go nearly to your papa's grave on the west–that far in every direction."

"Maybe you could get it so his grave would be on our land," she said.

"Maybe I could. It depends on where the section lines are, you see. I don't know much about this land business, but I aim to start finding out."

"If we had that much land," she said, "looks like we could nearly have our own country. There wouldn't nobody ever need to come around our house, and we could live just like we are now forever."

"We might even build a fence around the whole four sections some time," he said.

"A fence?" she said. "Wouldn't that take a whole lot of willow poles?"

"Oh Mary Dove," he said.

They laughed.

"We never will get through the things I don't know," she said.

"I hope we never do," he said. He explained as well as he could what a barbed-wire fence was.

"Does it hurt the animals?" she asked.

"No," he said. "Not unless there's some kind of a accident, like with a locoed horse or something."

She was thoughtful a minute or two, then said, "We'll get one. We'll build a fence all around, and never let nobody in except us, and our children when we have 'em, and maybe they'll find somebody to love and we'll let them come in. But that will be the thing: love. We won't never let nobody in that don't love everybody else. Then there won't be any troubles, like you've told me about, and everybody will always be happy."

"What a dreamer you are, Mary Dove," he said. He wanted to laugh at her again, but a lump came in his throat, and he was afraid to try laughter, for fear it would turn to tears.

3

As spring came on, they were planning for Red's trip to town. One day when they were sitting on the arbor bench in the sunshine, Mary Dove said, "Red, that old black hen wants to set so bad. Do you reckon you could bring home a rooster?"

They had built a small rock chicken house already, and Mary Dove was anxious to get a flock started.

"I'll try to bring a rooster," Red agreed.

"It don't hardly seem like spring," Mary Dove said, "without a bunch of little chickens running around the place."

"Well, if I can't bring everything," he teased, "which would you rather I'd bring you—a rooster or a new pair of shoes?"

"Why a rooster, Red, of course," she said. "You can make me another pair of shoes."

"I meant that for a joke," he said, "but you're right–we need a rooster more'n nearly anything."

"A lot depends on this trip to town," Mary Dove said.

Red didn't answer for a little while, but he was thinking it was time to tell her that more depended on it than she knew.

It had been arranged before he left the Plains ranch in the fall that by the first of April the boss would have a letter waiting for him at the post office in town, with instructions as to what he would have to do next. He knew he might have to leave Mary Dove for a while: at best he might have to go to the area roundup, but he wouldn't be surprised if he got orders to move to some ranch halfway across the state or in New Mexico. He worked for an outfit that was always spreading out or trying something new. He didn't know what he would do if they told him to leave the Badger Creek range, for he badly needed to work for wages at least another year. He decided there wasn't any use in worrying Mary Dove about that part, but it was time to tell her that he might have to be away from her for a few weeks at least.

"More depends on the trip than I've let you know," he said.

She listened carefully to what he told her, and said then, "I do understand about how much we need the money they pay you, and I guess I can bear whatever you have to do. You will come back here before you go anywhere else, won't you?"

"Yes," he said, "whatever orders I get, I'll come back here first."

"Well then," she said, "I just won't think any farther ahead than you coming back from town, and bringing me my rooster."

He could see there were tears in her eyes, but she had turned to him smiling. He grabbed her and kissed her and said to her, "Mary Dove, you are the sweetest wife that any man could ever have."

In a few days, not knowing for sure what the date was,

Red decided he had better go. "I ought to get that letter, if it's waiting for me," he said, "and if it's not, then I might wait a day or two for it, so if I don't get back when you expect me don't worry."

"I won't worry, Red," said Mary Dove.

The day before he left, Mary Dove went with him to see about the cows.

As they circled the herd, riding along the ridge above the shallow bowl where it was grazing, they could look for miles in every direction.

"Look a-yonder," Mary Dove suddenly said, pointing southward. "It's that smoke."

It was in the same place; it looked like the same smoke. It looked, Red knew now, like smoke from a chimney—from a fire in some kitchen where somebody was cooking dinner. "Good Lord," he said.

"Does it worry you, Red?" she asked him.

"No," he lied, "it don't worry me. But I reckon it does mean somebody's staying around awhile. Might be them settlers we was expecting is coming in already. But all it means to me right now is I want you to be extra careful. Don't get too far from the dugout, and whatever you do, don't let nobody in."

"You don't think nobody would hurt me, do you, Red?"

"No," he said firmly. "No, I don't think so, and you mustn't be scared. We just don't want to get mixed up with nobody, that's all."

He wondered if he ought to tell her what he thought a man might do—especially if, unlike Red, he understood the meaning of the color of her skin. But that was something he couldn't say to her yet, couldn't bear to have her know. Oh, he understood old Pardue now.

"Well, I'll try to mind you better than I done Papa," she said.

"Yes, it's just like when your papa used to go to town," Red said. "Just do like you done then, and don't worry."

He said it to her again the next morning at daybreak, just before he rode away. "Don't worry, Mary Dove."

"I ain't worrying, Red," she said, and kissed him. "Just hurry back to me, that's all."

She never even cried when he left her. He thought he was nearer crying than she was. "She don't hardly know enough to cry, pore little thing," he said to himself.

Birds were waking up around him as he rode, taking a southerly way. In the east the sky had faded to a gray clear as glass, through which two dim stars shone, but quickly, while he watched, color came into the scene. Flame-colored little clouds came like arrowheads shooting ahead of the sun, proclaiming it, and when it rose they vanished. He hoped Mary Dove was watching; he would remember to ask when he got home.

The sun would be the least bit later coming up where she was, for he had ridden out onto the level land of the Divide. Somewhere west of him, the direction he would be generally going, there must be a camp or a dugout, and he was looking for the smoke. He would like to know where that smoke came from, but he wouldn't like to approach it too closely, either. Presently he saw it, snaking up, white-looking against the dark side of the sky. Whatever it came from was lost among low trees or bushes. He kept it in view, circling south of it.

Looking toward the smoke, he failed to see a rider coming from the north until he heard him holler "Hey!"

Red slowed to wait for him. "Howdy," he called back.

The man was dressed like a farmer, in faded blue shirt and ducking britches, and he carried a shotgun the way a man would if he was out trying to get a few doves or a rabbit for dinner before he started his day's work.

"You just passing through?" the man asked Red.

"Not exactly," Red said. "I been camped out over yonder with a bunch of cows all winter." His gesture took in half the earth.

"Is that so?" the man said. "I been here since fall, myself, and never guessed there was a soul in the country. Been so busy trying to get some improvements started that I never prowled around very much."

"You live over there?" Red pointed toward the smoke.

"Yeah. Built me a little old shedroom and dugout till I could do better. With the houseful I got, I better not wait too long to do better." He laughed at his joke.

"You got a bunch of younguns?" Red asked.

"Six of 'em, and every one girls. Can you beat that?" the man said. "Say, you better come home with me and get some breakfast. My old lady and the gals'd be tickled to see you."

"I better go on," Red said. "I'm due in town early, and I got started late."

"Well now, when you get back here, you come and take a meal with us. Our name's Munden, and we'll be glad to get acquainted."

Red told his name. "I'm halfway expecting the boss to send me off somewhere clear out of the country," he said, "but if I get back here I'll take you up on that invitation."

"Now don't forget that," the man said. "You come and look my gals over some time—but remember about this thing when you do." He lifted his shotgun slightly, laughing happily. "I look after my gals."

"I don't blame you for that, Mr. Munden," Red said, riding off. "Glad I run into you."

"I'll be seeing you," said Mr. Munden.

Red imagined that if he got back there, and kept on living in that country very long, then sooner or later, Mr. Munden would. There wouldn't be any way around it. He would have to be figuring out what lies he could tell.

4

Sitting around being lonesome wouldn't hurry Red back. Having sat on the arbor bench watching the sun come up while she thought of Red watching it too, Mary Dove told herself that. The corn and beans might well have been planted already, but they had put that job off because there was always something else needing to be done. Mary Dove guessed Red didn't really like that kind of work; it would be a good surprise for him if she had it all done when he got home.

Getting the ground ready took all of the first day, and she was so tired when night came that she didn't lie awake missing Red. The next day she finished the planting well before sundown, and it was hard to keep from starting to look for him. Her father never had come home from town any sooner than late on the second night, and of course Red had said he might take a day or two longer. But then—he might come home faster than her papa had ever done, might think he had reason to.

Mary Dove went and bathed in the pool, combed out her hair and braided it and pinned it around her head—the way Red had showed her once, but she didn't always do. She put on a fresh dress, a blue print he liked, and cooked enough supper for him. But of course she had to eat it by herself, and darkness came and a late moon rose, and still he hadn't come.

For a long time she sat outside playing the guitar and singing. She felt so restless she didn't think she could go to bed, and when at last she knew she would go to sleep in spite of herself, she went and brought her bed out under the arbor. "I just don't want to go back in the dugout till he comes," she decided.

So she heard him call—though she had been asleep—and by the time he was swinging down from his saddle she was running to meet him. They were kissing and hugging by the time he hit the ground.

"Did you get everything, Red?" she asked him in a little while.

"I reckon I did," he said. He handed her a tow sack. "Here's your present, but be careful with it."

It was heavy, and something stirred in it. "It's my rooster!" she cried.

"He ain't in too good shape, after his trip," Red said. "Why don't you put him in the dugout till morning?"

While she put the rooster inside and set out some corn and water for him, Red unloaded the rest of the things, and they put up the horses together.

"I got you something else," he told her then. "I don't know if you can see 'em good enough by the moonlight."

"Oh, I think I can, Red. Let me see."

He picked up a package from a pile of stuff he had put near the door and handed it to her. "Don't say I never give you nothing," he said.

"Oh Red, it's shoes! I know it's shoes."

She tore the paper from them, and went out into the full moonlight holding them in her outstretched hands. They were made out of soft, smooth leather, with little round heels and high laced tops.

"They're so pretty," she said, "I may just set 'em up and look at 'em, and keep wearing the ones you made me."

"I want to see you wearing 'em," he said, "but I can wait till morning. I got some more stuff to show you then–listen, I even got you a side saddle; you won't have to wear them old britches all the time."

"Oh Red, how could you get so much?"

"I had some money waiting for me."

"And your letter?"

"Yes, I got my letter too. I'll tell you all about it in the morning, but I'm just too tired tonight."

"I bet you're hungry, too."

"No, not hungry. I eat some stuff coming along. I just want to get to bed."

"I moved a mattress outside. You want to sleep out here?"

"Anywhere," he said.

She went and got the other mattress and fixed their beds together. Soon they were snuggled close together under the blanket, for in early spring the nights still turned cool.

"I thought you was tired," she said presently.

"Not that tired," he said.

And that was the way they came back together after their first separation.

"Are you fixing to go off and leave me again?" was the first thing she asked him next morning.

"It's gonna be all right," he said. "I'll tell you all about my letter, but let's get some breakfast first."

"I reckon you're hungry this morning," she said.

She went and opened the dugout door, to go and fix some breakfast, and the rooster jumped right out in her face.

She gave a little cry. "Why I nearly forgot you," she said.

The first thing he did was fly up on the bench and give a good strong crow.

"He got over his trip, looks like," said Red.

The sun struck rich colors in his great drooping tail.

"Ain't that the prettiest tail you ever seen in your life?" Mary Dove cried. "I got to go and let the hens out."

She ran to the little rock chicken house and opened the door, calling, "Come and see what Red brought you."

They came out slowly, with little questioning clucks. The rooster took a look at them and crowed again.

"Are you gonna fix my breakfast, or are you gonna wait for them to get acquainted?" Red asked.

Mary Dove laughed. "Oh I'm coming, Red," she said. She ran and kissed him. "Me and the hens shore do thank you for bringing us a rooster."

"Much obliged, I'm sure," he said. He turned to the stack of supplies he had brought. "This here's some sausage I thought'd taste good," he said. "We got to get us a pig soon as we can, and raise some of our own." He pulled out another package. "I got some coffee, too."

Finally, after breakfast, when he was drinking the last of the coffee Mary Dove made, he told her about his letter.

"It ain't the best news in the world," he said, "but it's gonna be all right."

He wasn't fixing to have to go off anywhere, he said, not even to the roundup. The thing that would make the most difference in the lives of Red and Mary Dove was that another man was coming to work with Red. The Bar Diamond was preparing to establish a new ranch (already referred to in the letter as the Badger Creek Ranch), and the boss wanted Red and his partner to hold the herd there during the summer and start building some barns and corrals, getting ready for more cattle to be brought in the next fall.

"You'll have to stay and work over there at that camp now, won't you?" Mary Dove said. "And I won't get to go with you and help you, I guess."

"Looks like I'll just about have to go back and live over there for a while," Red said.

"I thought you wasn't gonna have to go off and leave me."

"Well, I ain't going far, and seems like I could manage somehow to see you every few days. But you see, Mary Dove, I can't let Jack Ryan know I'm living off over here with a woman."

"Jack Ryan?"

"That's his name. I know him, he's been here before. Come with me and stayed a little while at Badger Creek the first year. He's a good old boy. But you see, Mary Dove, I just can't afford to let him know about you."

He had said it twice. She guessed she saw. "When is he coming, Red?" she asked.

"It'll be about the first of May, according to the letter. He's got to go to the roundup, and see about some other things before he comes. I'll have time to get things ready for him —make it look like I've been staying over there at Badger Creek all the time." He planned on being able to live with Mary Dove for maybe a month longer, coming home to her nights. He could leave a note at the camp in case Jack got there sooner than he expected, telling him he'd gone off to camp somewhere else temporarily.

He was thinking about how he would manage. Mary Dove sat quietly wondering.

"Red," she said at last, "can't nobody ever know about me, as long as we live?"

To Red this was not a new question. "Oh, they'll have to, they'll have to sometime," he said. "I'll get things figured out so they can. But if Jack saw you now, and started asking questions, it couldn't cause nothing but trouble."

"Well," she said. "But can we help it?"

He explained that he meant to move the herd over in the other direction from Badger Creek, where there was water and good grazing. "We'll be kept pretty busy around camp, and I doubt if Jack ever comes over this away a-tall. If he ever sees the dugout he won't have to know there's a woman anywheres. I'll tell him some tale about a old sheepherder, and if you don't wander around too far from home I don't think he'll ever guess you're here."

"But you'll come?"

"Of course," he said. "I'll find excuses to get away. Shore 'nough, Mary Dove, it'll be all right for a little while; and this fall when I get my wages I'll quit and start getting a place of our own fixed up."

"Did you find out how to get the land?"

"I found out what I've got to do, but I figured I'd better come on home this time. Having the dugout and all here already will give us a claim to it, so I don't think we'll have any trouble."

"Oh Red, everything will be all right–won't it?"

"Of course it will be all right." He wondered how many times he had said that, to himself and then to Mary Dove, since he got the boss's letter. "Everything will be fine."

5

They began to live a new way then, for Red was gone all day doing work Mary Dove couldn't share.

"Why can't I go to the camp with you, Red?" she asked him the first day he went.

"You wouldn't know how to do the kind of stuff I got to do there," he said.

"Couldn't I just go?"

"No," he said. "Jack might come earlier than I'm expecting him, or some of them new settlers might come by. Badger Creek's a lot closer to where they're living than we are here."

He hadn't told her about the settlers before.

"I guess there's somebody living over there where we saw that smoke," she said.

"Yes," he said, "I saw the man. Munden's his name. He's built a dugout and a shack and I reckon he's fixing to farm."

"Has he got a family?"

"A wife and six kids."

"Did he say if they're boys or girls?"

"They're girls, every one of 'em."

"I wonder how old they are."

"I don't know, he didn't say." Red had a pretty good idea that some of them, at least, might be grown, and he wondered why he didn't tell Mary Dove that. He didn't have any kind of interest in girls that could make her jealous, and she wouldn't know how to begin being jealous if he did. He just didn't want to talk about the Munden family.

But he couldn't keep from thinking about them. As he worked with the cattle, moving them in the direction of Munden's place, the other side of Badger Creek, he often saw their smoke and thought about what might finally come of having these new neighbors. Sometimes he did nothing but sit around camp, keeping fires going to try to make it look like a place where somebody had been living for six months, and then there wasn't much to do but think. He began to be anxious for Jack Ryan to get there, with full instructions about the work they were to do. Rather than struggle all day with the mixed-up ideas in his brain, Red thought he would even welcome Jack's stories about the female companionship he discovered wherever he went.

Jack was known as a ladies' man by Bar Diamond hands everywhere. He was a dancy little Irishman, with curly black hair and dark blue eyes, and Red had never seen a girl that didn't take to him. Nor had he ever seen Jack remain satisfied very long before he discovered some girl in riding distance of wherever he happened to be.

So thinking one day, as he watched a fire he didn't need, the solution to one of Red's problems came suddenly clear in his mind. "The Munden girls!" he cried aloud.

He would sic Jack on the Munden sisters and, if the girls were as old as Red thought they must be and looked any better than a mud fence, Jack never would have time to be poking around finding Mary Dove's dugout.

"Everything's gonna be all right," Red jubilantly assured himself.

After a few weeks had passed he told Mary Dove that if he failed to come home some night she would know the new partner had got there.

"This summer's work will soon be over," he said to her, "and then we can live like we want to again."

"We can go back to our old way," she said.

One evening towards sundown, as Red was coming from the little creek valley where the herd now grazed, he saw a horse and rider on a far hilltop and knew that Mary Dove would sleep alone that night.

He rode to meet Jack, who greeted Red profanely and affectionately, as was his style, then said, "Say, you ain't looking too good."

"I'as sick awhile this winter," Red said.

"That's the bad thing about laying out by yourself," Jack said. "I reckon you never seen a soul all winter."

Red let that pass. They were riding in sight of the herd, and he gestured towards it.

"Fat, ain't they?" Jack said.

"Fat and gentle," Red said. "This has been a easy job."

"We'll have a little more to do now," Jack said. He went on and told Red more about the jobs laid out for them to do that summer: using rocks, brush, and poles—whatever materials they could find at hand—they were to build corrals and sheds enough to take care of another herd, a big one, and a string of horses. They were supposed to pick a site that would be good for a house and barns later on and begin to prepare it for building.

After supper they sat by the fire, wanting the warmth after sundown, and drank thick sweet coffee from rusty tin cups.

"Bar Diamond ain't getting in too soon," Jack said. "This country's settling up."

"Shore 'nough?" Red said.

"I come by a store and blacksmith shop about ten or fifteen miles west of here," Jack said.

"Well, I never knowed that," Red said. "That store would've come in handy."

"It's right new," Jack said. "There was a couple of houses close by, and looked to me like signs of settlers two or three places between here and there."

"There's a feller living not far from here," Red said, "but I never seen 'im till a few weeks ago when I'as on my way to town."

He told about old man Munden and his gals, not forgetting the part about the shotgun.

Jack laughed. "We'll have to see about that," he said.

"I figured you'd think so," Red said.

Jack got to telling then about a trip he made up to Mobeetie and an encounter with some dance-hall girls there, and that led him on to speak of other girls he had found here and there on the Stakéd Plains. Red could listen easily to those familiar-sounding tales and still give his mind to the picture of Mary Dove waiting and watching, not having given up yet the hope that he would come.

6

Mary Dove hadn't been prepared for the feeling that came to her, after Red had been gone for three days, that everything in the world she could ever care about had been taken away.

When Red went to town, even though she knew he might get a letter sending him off for a while, she had kept herself from being very lonesome. Now each day that passed without him seemed to deepen some unreasonable dread that had come upon her. She couldn't get rid of the notion that some lasting change, which she couldn't name or explain to herself, had taken place in their lives.

She needed to accept it, to understand it, or at least to find some consolation for it, and so she decided on a visit to the deep pool, seeking the old help she had known there. It was just past midday when she came there, and the sun shone into the depths of the water leaving only the bank beneath the cottonwoods and willows in the shade. Even there bright little yellow flowers glowed like sunbeams caught in the grass, and from thick branches unseen birds sent forth bursts of music. Amid that warmth and joy, only the dove seemed to mourn.

"You're not really sad," Mary Dove said. "You can't fool me. I see your mate right over there, waiting."

But the dove insisted on lonesomeness. "You've mourned all your life," said Mary Dove. "I wonder what *you* lost."

No more than anyone else, was what she thought. Doves always undertook to do the mourning for the whole world.

Yet the dove's note prevailed. To get away from it, Mary Dove went quickly down into the pool, without any waiting in the sunshine. The cool caress of the sunlit green water soothed her, but she waited in vain for it to wash away the sadness.

Sooner than usual, she tired of swimming. Maybe, she thought, the trouble was just that she was tired. Her body felt heavy when she pulled herself out of the water, and she lay still awhile on the rock, letting the sun dry her.

When she sat up she noticed a thickening of her waist that at first she wondered about, but then she thought of some other changes that had taken place in her lately and suddenly she knew the cause of it all. "I *was* heavy," she exclaimed aloud. "I'm going to have a baby!"

She stayed sitting on the rock as the full sense of her discovery came slowly clear and the tiredness and sadness went out of her. In their place came a new delight, different from anything she had ever known, and she believed it was what she had come to the pool to find. Red said they would have a baby when the Lord was ready for them to, and he was ready now. She had not found God's presence at the pool in the way she expected, but she had a message from him anyway.

As she went back to the dugout, she began to be impatient to tell her news. "If only Red would come home tonight," she said–but though she missed him, the old dread lonesomeness no longer possessed her. She felt linked–joyfully linked–to everything alive in the world.

"You ain't the only ones," she said to the setting hen and the rooster, when she went to the chicken house to scatter corn.

"Don't feel so proud of yourself," she said to the cow, who was already swelling with the calf one of Red's bulls had given her. "Me and Red's gonna have a baby, too."

She could hardly wait to tell Red. She knew he thought it would be good if they didn't have a baby right away, but as soon as he knew he had started new life that was growing inside her, he just couldn't help being glad.

"How will it be?" she wondered and wondered. "I'll get big," she knew, "maybe too big to wear the clothes I have."

But she would think of something to do about that. There would have to be clothes for the baby—where did people get baby clothes, what kind did babies need? Red had said it wasn't as easy as she imagined for a woman to have a baby. But why not? What was she supposed to do? She really couldn't believe the birth of her baby could be much different from the dropping of a calf, but Red would surely know. If he didn't, he would find out.

If she had known any other women—could have married Red by the law of the land as well as the law of God, and his sisters had been her sisters—they would surely have helped her. This was part of what she once dreamed of, but if it couldn't be, why then as long as she had Red she wouldn't worry. He was all she needed: father and mother and sister, as once he promised her, and all the world besides.

She just couldn't wait to tell him.

7

Red meant it when he told Mary Dove he would be seeing her every few days. It was easy then to picture himself telling Jack Ryan he was fixing to ride off over yonder—somewhere—for some purpose—might not be back for a while.

In fact, when the time came, he could not think of any explanation to offer Jack that didn't sound silly or suspicious. In desperation he wondered sometimes what would happen if he simply told the truth.

"What truth?" he said to himself then. Would he say to Jack, "I believe I'll take off awhile tonight, and go and visit my wife"?

"And when did you marry a wife?" Jack would say.

"Why on Christmas Eve," he would answer. "Standing on a hill at sundown, with seven sheep for witnesses."

He might as well say at once, "I'm keeping a mulatto woman

over yonder in a dugout, and I reckon I'll go sleep with her tonight."

There would be no question in Jack's mind about the truth. It wouldn't bother him, either. If Red had found him a woman, and for some reason couldn't marry her or didn't, that would be Red's business. Even the color of her skin wouldn't make any difference to Jack, as long as Red had sense enough to keep her in her place. And Jack would never put a hand on a woman that belonged to a pal of his–Red didn't need to worry about that.

Well, he had fooled himself then, and fooled Mary Dove. It would be better, surely, to go and tell her so–hear her ask him, her big believing eyes bright with tears, "Is that really the truth, Red? Wasn't we ever really married?"

"No, it's a lie!" he would have to shout then, and put his arms around her and shelter her forever against the world that wouldn't take her as his wife.

Jack said to him late one afternoon when they had been working together almost a week, "I don't much believe you're over that sick spell yet. You ain't acting like yourself."

"I'm all right," Red said.

"What would be good for both of us," Jack said, "is a little change of scenery. Why don't we just take off this evening and go see them sisters?"

"I don't know–" Red said.

"Well, if you don't feel like it we can wait awhile."

But of course Red knew he would have to go with Jack a few times, to get him strung in. The sooner the better, he thought. "Oh let's go," he said, and they quit and got ready.

They rode up hailing the house from a distance, as the custom was in that country then. The sun, going down, blazed in the single narrow window of the little lean-to room. A woman with an ample white apron settled over her broad hips and belly came to the door and stood on the rock step wiping her hands on something, waiting for them to get off their horses and approach her.

"Howdy ma'am," said Jack, stepping ahead. "Have I got the pleasure of speaking to Mrs. Munden?"

"I reckon you have," she said doubtfully. "My man's off over yonder. He'll be back dreckly."

"I talked to him about a month ago, Mrs. Munden," Red said then. "My name's Red Jones. This here's Jack Ryan."

"Well, come in, Red and Jack," she said acceptingly, and turning called, "Girls, it's that feller Papa told us about."

As Red and Jack stepped inside, young girls started popping up out of the earth floor.

Mrs. Munden laughed at their look of astonishment. "I guess they look about like a family of ground squirrels coming out of their hole," she said. "It's the entrance to our dugout–the girls sleeps down there."

They stood in a row along one end of the room. Four of them looked about grown, one around twelve, the youngest nine or ten. Mrs. Munden told off their names, oldest to youngest as she explained: Lizzie, Sallie, Maggie, Effie, Hattie, Nettie. Each in her turn said howdy. They appeared to be nice looking girls, but no lamp had been lit and it was hard to be sure just what they looked like.

"Hattie and Nettie, run and find Papa," Mrs. Munden said. "Boys, set down and let me fix you some supper."

"We done had supper, Mrs. Munden," Jack assured her. "What we'as hungry for tonight was company, and Red said Mr. Munden had invited him to visit."

"We're tickled to have visitors," Mrs. Munden said. "It was a long, lonesome winter, but you know there's two new families living in visiting distance, just come in the last few weeks. Now what do you think about that?"

"I'm a little surprised to hear it," Red said. "It's not the time of year you look for settlers."

"No, it ain't," Mrs. Munden agreed. "But these folks was fixed so's they didn't have to wait to get a crop out. There's a young man, says he aims to farm, and his pa, that's fixing to bring in a herd of sheep."

Mrs. Munden pulled cane-bottomed chairs out from the table for Red and Jack to sit in. "Light the lamp, Lizzie," she told the oldest girl. Then she and the girls sat together on a long homemade bench.

The girls all looked a lot like their mother, Red thought, or at least they all had brown hair pulled back from their faces. Lizzie had more of a slender face than the others, a solemn face. Another one of them–Sallie, he thought–had lighter, wavier hair and a rounder, more smiling face.

The two youngest came then bringing in their father, who shook hands with the boys and declared he couldn't tell when he had been so glad to see anybody.

"Mrs. Munden says, though, that some more folks has moved in," Red said. "A feller with some sheep, she says."

Mr. Munden misunderstood his interest in the sheep. "Well, now, you don't want to worry about that," he said. "He ain't a big sheep man, ain't apt to interfere none with your cows."

"No, I don't expect so," Red said. "Whereabouts is he settling?"

"He's filed on some land just off of the Divide, joining his boy's claim on the flat land. He said he might have looked farther and done better, maybe got a little better water on his place, but they wanted their land to join."

"I don't blame 'em for that," Red said. (He wouldn't be very close to Mary Dove.)

"We'll have to get everybody together pretty soon–have some kind of a to-do," Mrs. Munden said.

"That'd be mighty nice, Mrs. Munden," said Jack, letting a long look travel down the length of the bench where the girls were sitting.

Mrs. Munden wanted to know where the boys had come from and what kind of families they had left behind. Red told about his five sisters and how in their manners and the differences in their ages the Munden girls reminded him of them, and she said, "Now don't that beat it? You come and see my girls whenever you get to feeling homesick."

Jack said, "I ain't got no sisters, Mrs. Munden. Can I come too?"

"Bless your heart," she said, "you come too, and the girls will make it up to you."

"I'll be a brother to them," Jack said, and everybody laughed.

Mr. Munden slapped Jack on the back. "That's the ticket," he said. "I won't need to get out the old shotgun, at that rate."

"Now Papa," said Mrs. Munden. "Don't talk that away before the girls."

The girls on the bench looked prim, and the subject was changed, but there was in the air the feeling of mutual and satisfying understanding. For the rest of the visit, the men did most of the talking, but the views of the women were clear. If either one or both of the boys ever wanted to come a-courting, they wouldn't be turned away.

As they started to leave, Mrs. Munden said, "If we'as back home I'd tell you boys to come and go to preaching with us Sunday and take dinner afterwards. I reckon we won't have no preaching, but y'all come and eat with us anyway."

They accepted the invitation, but Red expected that something was liable to happen to keep him from going, when the time came.

As they rode back to camp, Jack said, "I'm staking my claim on that little old blue-eyed Sallie–which un do you favor?"

"I'll have to look 'em over some more," Red said.

"That Lizzie's took a shine to you," Jack said.

"You got a good imagination," Red answered.

8

One midmorning Mary Dove sat singing under her arbor, half shaded from the strong May sun. Now, as she cradled the guitar against her, it was easy to feel how her belly was swelling.

She liked the feel—not the promise it offered or the pleasure it recalled, or at least she was not thinking of these things. She was not thinking at all, only knowing herself strong with life as an egg or a swelling seed, and nothing more asked of her than of them. Gradually, she stopped singing words, not caring to take the trouble to recall and form them, and simply hummed softly from time to time as a sun-warmed insect might do, and plucked out of the big strings on her guitar sounds that she felt deep in her body more clearly than she heard them with her ears.

Some days she could sit that way for hours, never missing Red at all. It was usually toward night that she began to be anxious, and wondered and wondered what kept him away.

So she never saw him until he was almost upon her. Then she laid down the guitar and went to him, and they came together embracing, without a word.

"You've still got our beds out here," he said in a little while, when they stood apart.

"Yes," she said.

"We'll talk after while," he said, "but I can't stay very long."

"All right," she said.

It was only after he had satisfied his need for her that Red realized there had been a difference in the way her body felt to him. He turned to her lying now a little apart from him, flat on her back, unmoving except for the slow rise and fall of her softly rounded belly. And that of course told the difference: it had been flat as a shingle till now. Her breasts, that had been so small and firm, were full and womanly.

Mary Dove was with child. His child. His bastard, nigger child. He lay struck still by that fact, by those words, for a time he couldn't tell the length of, before it came to him to wonder whether Mary Dove knew. Surely she did, surely she must, and yet no one had ever told her anything. He remembered a time he had put off her questions—he had not been to her all the things he once promised. It was possible she hadn't guessed what he had planted inside her.

At last, with great effort, he spoke her name.

"Yes, Red," she answered.

"Mary Dove, do you know—can you tell—" he felt himself flushing as he stammered; he broke off and flatly said, "Oh Mary Dove, you are going to have a baby."

She turned to him, radiant and smiling. "I'm so glad you know it, Red," she said to him. "I was trying and trying to think how to tell you, but it's a whole lot better this way."

"You're glad about it," he said wonderingly.

"How would I not be?" she said.

"What will we do with it?" he asked.

"What people do," she said. "I guess I will feed it like the cow does her calf—that's right, ain't it?"

"Oh yes, Mary Dove, that's right. But there's so many things."

"I've been thinking of 'em," she said. "What to do about clothes for it—but you can find out, can't you, Red, and go and get some for us?"

He could see a picture of himself going to Mrs. Munden and asking for advice about baby clothes.

"Red, you're not glad," Mary Dove said, suddenly understanding him.

"It's only that I wish it hadn't happened for a little while longer," he said to her. "Till we're better settled and know for sure how we can manage things."

"It'll be all right," she said, nestling against him. "Having a baby to love can't help but be all right."

He drew her close and kissed her. He hoped she would think that was an answer.

"I can't stay much longer now," he said. He got up and began to put on his clothes. "Jack went off to eat dinner with them new settlers, and I told him I was feeling sick and couldn't go with him. But I'll have to be back when he gets in, you see, or he'll start to suspicion something."

She sat up and pulled on her shift, watching him thoughtfully. "Couldn't you just come?" she asked. "Do you have to tell him things?"

Having dressed, he sat on the bench and looked down at her sitting cross-legged on the bed, as a little girl might. He felt, as he had at times from the first, like her father: like someone sent to take the place of Pardue.

"Yes, Mary Dove, I've got to tell him things," Red said. "When you're working with a feller, camping out with him away off from anywheres, you don't just ride off to be gone half a day without giving him some explanation."

"Lying to him?"

"Yes, if that's what's called for."

"Have people got to tell lies sometimes, Red?" she asked.

"Sometimes," he said. "Sometimes it's the only way to keep from hurting somebody."

"Hurting their feelings, you mean?"

"Sometimes that."

"That was why you lied to me about the cows that time."

"Yes, that was it. And now lying's the only way I can see to take care of you, keep folks from finding out about you and maybe sending you off somewhere away from me."

"Could they do that?"

"They might."

"Who would? Them new settlers?"

"Anybody might, I don't know."

"Have you seen 'em, Red? Are they mean?"

"No, they ain't mean. They're just ordinary folks. I went with Jack to see 'em because I wanted him to get interested in visiting them. I thought maybe there might be a girl he'd take up with, so he wouldn't have time to come prowling around and find you."

"If they ain't mean why would they hurt us?"

"Because they would think it was the right thing to do."

"How could they think that?"

"Oh Mary Dove, I've tried and tried to tell you how people

would think about us. I don't know what else to say, and I haven't got time to go through it all again now."

She looked down. He guessed there were tears in her eyes. "Are you mad at me, Red?" she asked him.

He bent and kissed her. "No," he said. "You couldn't know about all that stuff, and I'm not mad. But I've got to go."

"I wish you was a little bit glad about the baby," she said as he straightened and turned away.

"I am, Mary Dove."

"But I don't want you to lie about it."

"I'm glad for your sake, Mary Dove."

She let him go without protest, as she always had done.

He half turned back, wanting to give some assurance, but there was nothing he could say about the baby that she would want to hear.

He rode fast at first, leaving there, getting away. But then the thoughts he had been holding off came down upon him, and he rode ever more slowly, bowed under their weight, lacking strength to try to set them in order.

Voices came from far back in his childhood. "Don't you even know how people make babies?" one tauntingly said. He caught himself trying to answer it, defend himself. But if he hadn't, why had the discovery of a child conceived been such a shock to him? That was a present he shouldn't be surprised to find he'd given.

That same voice from childhood came speaking low in some closed-up, secret place, telling secret stories. Telling a tale he had heard more than once: it had happened to several people in different places, or perhaps it was really all one.

The girl in the story was the prettiest girl in town but thought she was too good for any of the boys there. Then came a man from another state, most likely Louisiana. He had a curly mustache and shiny pointed boots, and he was the one she would have. Her mama and papa begged her, but she wouldn't listen to them. So she married the man of her choice, and by and by they had a little baby. And when the girl came to herself after it got born, and they brought it and showed it to her, she commenced screaming, and never stopped till she went clear out of her mind and they had to lock her up, and keep her so till this very day. For that baby was black as tar from head to toe. They came to find out that back in the Louisiana man's family, back so far he claimed to have forgotten it himself, there was somebody had to do with a Negro.

"And that's the way it goes: when there's nigger blood in a family, it'll be there forever and a solid black baby can always be born."

"Shut up!" cried Red.

Sangaree cocked his head. Red spoke to him. "No, it's all right, old boy, I ain't plumb crazy."

He didn't believe that tale anyway, never had. No child of his and Mary Dove's could be as black as tar.

Part-nigger bastard it would be though, and all the world would know it. His son would never thank him for his being. "Some favor you done me, getting me born," was what that son would say.

When he got back to camp he realized that it still wasn't much past dinner time. Jack would be gone a long time yet, might even stay for supper if the Mundens asked him to. Red could have stayed all day with Mary Dove, but then he had known that all along. He was not really as surprised at the time of day as he pretended to himself to be. He was not really surprised when he found that he was riding on toward the Mundens' place without even stopping at the camp. He could say he got to feeling better–and maybe, if he was around ordinary everyday people for a while, he really would.

Mrs. Munden seemed to have figured out a way to have the big get-together she had spoken of, Red thought. Dinner was evidently over, and there was a gang of people sitting outside in the shade, everyone looking toward him as he approached. He felt sheepish now, and wished himself back at camp again.

He tied his horse next to Jack's and walked toward the house. Mr. and Mrs. Munden both got up and came to meet him.

"I got to feeling better," he mumbled, but they both seemed so glad to see him that he didn't feel awkward very long.

"You getting here just puts the cap on the day," Mrs. Munden declared.

Mrs. Munden now undertook to make him acquainted with everybody. "Now let's see," she said, "you know Papa and the girls. Here's Mr. and Mrs. Johnson, that we told you about, and their son Mark and his wife, Dora. They got a drove of childern you'll see around here somewheres, too."

The men got up and shook hands. Clearly father and son, they were tall, thin men with browned faces and friendly blue eyes. Mrs. Johnson was little and spry, and her daughter-in-law was so heavy with child it was hard to imagine what she would look like when she wasn't.

(And Mary Dove would look like that, and then–he quickly turned away from Dora Johnson.)

"Now here's the one you couldn't have been expecting," Mrs. Munden was going on. "And neither was we, let me tell you. Remember I'as talking about how I wished we could have preaching? Well, we done had it once today, and fixing to again this evening. For we have got us a preacher."

She pointed triumphantly to the man now turned to greet Red. "Brother Michael," she loudly proclaimed.

The preacher was a tall pale man with thin pale hair that stuck out around his head as a light breeze blew through it. He put out his hand and said, "I'm glad to see you're feeling better, your friend said he had to leave you sick."

Red shook the hand and said, "I'm glad to know you, Brother," but he had trouble looking into the man's mild eyes (strange colored eyes, nearly honey-colored like his hair) and wondered how such gentle eyes could seem to look right through him.

Red wasn't used to feeling that way about preachers; and

in fact, though Brother Michael wore a long black coat and a black string tie and spoke in pulpit tones, he didn't seem quite like the preachers Red had known before. "But that's my guilty conscience," Red said to himself.

"Now you can talk to the preacher after while," Mrs. Munden said, taking Red by the arm. "I want you to go in the house now and let Lizzie get you something to eat. I bet you ain't had a bite all day."

"I don't know as I could eat," Red said.

"Course you could. You'll feel a lot better with something on your stomach; now you go on."

As if from far away, Red saw how the mother was helping the daughter to set her cap for the young man not yet spoken for. He followed Lizzie into the house and sat down in the chair she pulled out for him, still thinking about the scene as though it were something being showed to him out of another part of his life.

"Mr. Jones," Lizzie said sharply. He could tell she had spoken before.

"Miss Lizzie?" he said.

"Are you sure you're all right, not still sick?"

"I'm all right," he said.

"I was asking you if you like chicken." She was at the stove taking the lid off a big iron roaster. The smell of sage and onion dressing came to him as though through the years.

"It smells like home," he said. "Ain't nothing I like any better."

"Dressing don't make you sick?"

"Never did," he said.

"Well then." She brought a plate and set it before him. "Is that all right?" she asked.

"Fine, if you'll set and talk to me."

She pulled out a chair and sat down.

"You remind me of my oldest sister a little," Red said.

"I guess oldest sisters are always a lot alike," Lizzie said. "They get used to looking after the rest."

"Maybe it helps a girl when she gets some kids of her own," Red said. "My sister's got three, or maybe four by now–she's older than you, of course."

"I expect she's a good mother."

"She's got good kids," said Red. "I wish I could see 'em right now."

He hadn't thought much about his nieces and nephew–the two girls red-haired like his sister, the boy a sturdy tow-head–but now all of a sudden he did indeed wish he could see them. All of a sudden he believed he had always meant to go back and live close to them some day–with kids of his own growing up with their cousins. How much better than a lonely little shack on a cattle ranch would be the family home fixed up and painted, filled with aunts and uncles and cousins gathered for dinner and the house smelling of dressing and fresh-cut cedar.

"Have you?" Lizzie said, again being forced to repeat some question.

"Forgive me, Miss Lizzie," Red said. "Maybe I ain't feeling just right. My mind keeps wandering, and I was thinking about Christmas for some reason."

"Little uns makes you think of Christmas sometimes," Lizzie said. "I was wondering if you'd seen your sister's family for a while."

"It's been nearly two years," Red said.

"You ought to go back," she said.

"I wish I could," he said.

She didn't question him about that. He looked at her sitting across the table, erect and still-faced. She didn't seem to be a woman that talked when she didn't have anything to say. (It was funny but more than his sister, now, she reminded him of Mary Dove.)

The two little girls came in then. "Brother Michael's fixing to preach," one said, "soon as Red gets through eating."

"Not Red, Hattie," Lizzie scolded. "Mr. Jones."

"I wish you'd all call me Red," Red said.

"Is that what your sisters calls you?" the other little girl wanted to know.

"Yes, they do," Red said. "Nobody but my mother ever called me anything else, and she give up a long time ago and said Red, too."

"I want to hear the preaching," Nettie said.

"You ain't used to waiting for things, are you, Miss Nettie?" Red said.

"She's spoiled," Lizzie said.

"I know about youngest sisters, too," Red said.

He smiled at Nettie, and she came close and put a hand on his shoulder.

"Well, I'm nearly done now," he said. "I want to hear preaching, too, Miss Nettie. It's been a long time since I did."

"Now you girls run on," Lizzie said, "and let Red take his time. We got all evening to hear preaching."

The little girls went on out.

"There ain't nobody in such a hurry," Lizzie said. "Nettie just takes it into her head that she ought to have things her way."

"Whereabouts did you-all find a preacher?" Red asked.

"Mr. Johnson brought him," Lizzie said. "He had to go to town to make some arrangements about getting some sheep drove out here, and he met Brother Michael in the hotel where he stayed all night. Somebody had stole all the preacher's money, and he didn't have nowhere else to go, so when Mr. Johnson asked him if he'd like to come home with him and preach to just a handful of us settlers, Brother Michael said he figured the Lord had sent him for that very thing."

"It might be so," Red said. "Is Brother Michael a pretty good preacher?"

"He got us pretty well stirred up this morning," Lizzie said. "He preached on 'wherever two or three are gathered together' and I reckon he got the old folks to thinking about having a regular church."

"Folks needs a church," Red said.

"We'd all like it," Lizzie said.

Red soon finished eating, and they carried their chairs out into the yard to join the preacher's waiting audience. Brother Michael stood among them, the women sitting on chairs and benches and the men and children seated on the ground.

The text of the sermon now was "He that receiveth you receiveth me, and he that receiveth me receiveth him that sent me." The subject was rewards in heaven, with only a hint of the fiery punishment awaiting those who did not deserve such rewards.

Red thought it was decent of Brother Michael to preach that way, to the folks that had taken him in and fed him; but that was not the kind of sermon he had been brought up on.

Mrs. Munden seemed to feel the same way. After Brother Michael had finished his sermon and prayed, and then sat down among them, she said to him: "Brother Michael, that was a fine sermon, and it ain't for me to criticize the Lord's work, but it appears to me that you oughtn't to forget, wherever you go there's sinners to be preached to."

"Ah, Mrs. Munden, we're sinners all, and that's the truth," said Brother Michael. "There's the old Adam in us, every one, but by our repentance and the grace of God, we'll find our salvation."

"Amen!" cried old Mrs. Johnson.

"Sisters, you warm my heart," the preacher said. "I long for nothing more than to stand before a host of people, the saved and the unsaved, and pour out to them not only the promises of God but the certainty of eternal damnation to them that will not believe nor repent."

"Glory hallelujah!" Several of the ladies joined in that cry, including Lizzie Munden.

"If only we could have a good old-time revival meeting," Mrs. Munden said.

"Well now," old Mr. Johnson said. "I don't know why we couldn't. There's folks coming in all around us. I bet if we left word at Ralph Edwards's store we'd find out there's plenty of 'em would like to have a camp meeting."

There would be a camp meeting. Red could shut his eyes and see it springing up in some empty creek valley, the preacher standing against the sky on a hilltop like the one where he stood before God with Mary Dove. Red thought he could have seen it coming then if he had tried: some preacher like Brother Michael, no ordinary man, called to the wilderness to bring down God's wrath on the ones that had taken his laws in their own hands and molded them to suit their pleasure.

He became aware of Lizzie standing just behind him, leaning to speak low to him. "Jack and Sallie's aiming to go pick some flowers—Mama says they can go if we go with 'em."

"Fine," Red said, getting up.

Jack and Sallie, he saw, stood a little apart from the group of older folk. He went with Lizzie to join them.

"I'as getting restless, just listening to the old folks talking about a camp meeting," Sallie said.

"I'd just as soon think about something else awhile, too," said Red.

"But you'll come to the meeting?" asked Lizzie.

"Oh yes," Jack answered for him. "We wouldn't miss it, would we, Red?"

Red said he was sure they wouldn't. He knew he couldn't if he wanted to; there was something would have him there, and he only hoped it would bring him a way to see clear what he ought to do next.

The flowers, called black-eyed Susans by the Munden girls, were growing in a low spot—actually a wet-weather lake—about a half a mile south of the house. They made an object for a pleasant walk, long enough that when they returned with armloads of the rank-smelling weeds, the company was getting ready to leave.

Mrs. Munden stood near their wagon, which still had the

sheet over it from the trip west, saying some last words to them.

"Now you make Mark drive slow and look where he's going," she was saying to Dora Johnson. "We don't want nothing happening before it's supposed to."

"Don't worry, Mrs. Munden," Mark said. "I'm careful with my wife—don't know where I could find another one like her."

Red stood letting the heads of the flowers he carried trail in the dust. (Thinking Oh Lord. Mary Dove off over yonder not even knowing a woman is supposed to be careful. Running up and down the creeks, and no one to watch after her.)

"Red, look what you're doing," Lizzie said. "I don't believe you care very much about flowers."

He saw she was teasing. She probably expected a man to drag wild flowers in the dirt. She knew what had to be expected of a man. (But Mary Dove. Oh Lord, poor Mary Dove.)

It was a relief to Red to hear Jack say that it was time for them to head for camp. They got the invitation to supper that Red had expected, but the boys exchanged looks telling each other they knew when there had been enough of a good thing. They excused themselves.

"You boys come back ever' chance you get," Mrs. Munden said. "We'll have some more word about that camp meeting."

9

Although Red didn't tell Mary Dove much about the Munden sisters, she guessed them into a way of being that was as real to her as anything in the world beyond her creeks and hills could be. She pictured Red among them as among his own sisters at home, talking and laughing with them about things that never had to be explained.

They were all very fair and very tall, with hair like her father's, the color of dry grass in late summer. (She never imagined anyone else with hair the color of Red's; hair like a patch of flaming sunset sky was just his mark.) They were always together in a bunch like a covey of quails; and they moved from place to place as the blue quails did, with heads held high and unhurried little steps, for they could go anywhere they wanted to go and never care who saw them.

A few times at night (for now that she had to lie down alone sleep never came as quickly as it used to do), she thought about how it might be if the sisters some time went out walking (as people in songs often did) and wandered so far away from home they came to where they caught a glimpse of Mary Dove. Wouldn't they think, "There's a lonesome young girl, a pretty young girl, let's go and talk to her and take her home with us"? Wouldn't they come to her and kiss her and take her by the hand and lead her to their home?

She would be half falling asleep then, half dreaming how she let herself be led, and then something (some animal noise, it might be, or only her relentless sense of reality) would jerk her back to recollection of everything that Red had ever told her about the way the world would be for her, and she would know the answer. No. No, they wouldn't come to her or speak to her or ever touch her hand. She could see them clearly then, how they would be, drawing together like threatened quails and moving away from her, still with their heads in the air, and their little measured steps just quick enough that she could never catch them if she tried.

And there was Red in the midst of them, like a player in a singing party game.

She knew he was working all day and camping at night with his partner, but she couldn't get that picture out of her head. She was as certain as if she had followed him that he went to them the day he found out about the baby. It was what he would do, needing comfort Mary Dove could find no way to give.

Often she told herself that she would never learn. She had been silly to think Red would be as tickled about the baby as she was. She ought to have known that a baby coming now wouldn't tickle Red any, and if it looked very much like her, that would make things harder still. She ought to have thought of all this–Red must wonder if she ever would learn to think and do like the people he was used to living with.

Still, she couldn't help having the baby. And neither could she help being glad. She might as easily have felt sad because flowers bloomed or songbirds nested.

One day she noticed an algerita berry bush a-light with early morning sunshine. She had forgotten to watch for the berries ripening, and was so delighted at discovering them suddenly ripe that she went home at once to get a bucket to hold them and for an hour or so hardly thought of anything else, even the baby. They were so little (about half the size of her little fingernail) and so well protected by the stiff prickly leaves of the bush that it took a long time to gather as much as a mouthful. For a while she ate all she picked, then began trying to save some in the bucket. Her father had liked them with sugar and thick cream; she didn't much, but she had always gathered berries to take home and without thinking why meant to now.

She was sitting on the ground, reaching back into the center of the bush, when she heard Red holler.

"Hey Mary Dove!" he called, and she pulled back her hand and jumped up so fast that she scratched herself and knocked over her bucket. Not caring, she ran to him. He was walking toward her, having left Sangaree by the spring when he saw her on the slope above him.

She went into his arms and they kissed.

Then she gestured toward her overturned bucket. "Look what you done," she said, teasing. "You made me spill my berries." She held up her hand. "And scratched my hand, too." There was only a faint mark across it, though; it wasn't much of a scratch, but he took her hand and kissed it.

"You fixing to make jelly?" he asked then.

She shook her head. "I don't know nothing about jelly,"

she said. "Papa used to say them plums down the creek would make good jelly, but we didn't know what to do about it."

They were walking back to the berry bush. She went and picked up her bucket. "They're nearly all spilled," she said. "You want to eat these?"

"No thanks," he said. "I always thought they had kind of a sickly whang to 'em. The jelly ain't so bad."

"If I knew how I'd make some," she said. "Maybe you could ask them settler girls, I reckon they know how."

"They might," he said. "How come you to mention them?"

They were walking back toward the dugout now, going slowly, hand in hand.

"I think of them," she said simply.

They went and sat on the arbor bench, and he held her close against him. "I never meant to stay away so long," he said.

"You had to," she said.

There was nothing but acceptance in her voice. He would rather she had questioned him or scolded. She ought to say, "You could have found a way to come if you had really cared."

"It's been nearly two weeks," he said, having to accuse himself.

"I never tried to count the days," said Mary Dove.

"Every day I got up thinking I'd find some good excuse to get away from Jack, but we work close together all the time and there just ain't no chance."

"Did you think of a lie to tell today?"

"Oh Lord, Mary Dove, haven't you forgot what I said about that?"

"I remembered," she said. "I see why a lie might be better than the truth sometimes."

"Well it ain't. It might seem better, but it ain't right to lie. But yes, I thought of one. Or not really. I went to see about the cows, like I told Jack I would. Only I come on here. I don't know what I'll say when I get back, for he'll wonder why I was gone so long."

"I guess you can't stay long."

"I never can."

"Maybe you don't want to take the time up talking."

"We'll talk awhile."

"Then Red–if you have time to talk today–I wish you would tell about them sisters."

"What about 'em?" he asked.

"What do they look like? What do they do? Are they as old as me?"

"Well, there's six of 'em. The youngest one's nine or ten, and the oldest one's eighteen or nineteen I reckon. I don't know what they look like–they're just ordinary-looking girls."

"But Red–"

"Yes?"

"Girls ain't ordinary to me."

"Oh Mary Dove." He felt a familiar twisting of something in his breast.

"Do tell me, Red."

He sat up away from her, made himself smile. "Well then," he said. "The least gal's right feisty, used to getting her way. Her name is Nettie and they fix her hair in long curls. Next, there's Hattie. She's kind of a tomboy, kind of like you. She's got brown hair, straight. They've all got brown hair, some darker and some lighter, and I reckon they've all got blue eyes. The next four's all what you might call grown. At least my sisters called it that. I expect they're all looking for fellers. Effie and Sallie–Sallie's the next to the oldest–are lighter complected; Sallie's plumper than the rest. Maggie more or less keeps to herself–I haven't noticed her much. Lizzie's the oldest, and acts like it. Reminds me of my oldest sister, keeping an eye on the rest. There ain't any of 'em what you could call pretty girls, and the middle-sized uns have got spotty faces, but they're good-looking enough. Just ordinary girls, like I said."

"Oh, I wish I could see 'em," said Mary Dove. "Do you go to see 'em pretty often, Red?"

"Now what made you ask that?" he said.

"Oughtn't I to?" she asked him.

"No, it's all right," he said. "I have been to see 'em several times–on account of Jack, you know."

"I guess you like it too. I guess it's kind of like going home."

"Yes, that," he said. "And it's not just the Mundens, you see. There's two more families come in, both named Johnson –they're kinfolks–and a preacher that's been staying around and preaching some. I been to Sunday meeting twice."

"They ain't got no church house, have they?"

"No, Brother Michael just preaches at folks' houses."

"Does he preach about Jesus?"

"More about sin," Red said.

"Sin?" she said.

"Doing wrong," he said. "I'll tell you all about what the preacher says some day when we've got lots of time."

"Tell me about the Johnson people."

"There's a old couple, figuring on raising sheep. Their son's got land joining them, he's gonna farm. Has got a wife and a bunch of kids–one brand-new baby, born since they come. And listen, Mary Dove: what I'as gonna tell you. Seeing how she took care of herself made me think you might not know how a woman's supposed to do when she's fixing to have a baby. You mustn't run and jump around, the way you're used to doing. You might hurt yourself, or the baby, or both of you."

"Could I do that, Red?"

"Yes, you could."

"Could the baby die, before it even got born?"

"Yes," he said.

"I didn't know that," she said. "I'll be awful careful."

"I'll try to find out some more things for you, before the time comes."

"When do you reckon it'll be?" she asked.

"Fall, I guess," he said. "I don't know exactly. But everything will be all right, 'cause I'll be staying with you all time by then."

"Oh Red," she said, "will you ever really be again?"

"Of course I will," he said. "When summer's over, it will all be just the same."

10

Red stayed with Mary Dove too long. He had thought when he slipped away from camp he might only talk to her a little, tell her how to take care of herself, see if she needed any heavy jobs done around the place. He should have known better than that. Whatever he got to thinking as he listened to Brother Michael's words about repentance of sins, when Mary Dove was by his side she was his wife. Before he could repent of that sin, he would have to part from her forever.

He didn't bother to circle around and come in from the direction of the herd, as he had meant to do. He couldn't think of anything to say to Jack, no matter what direction he came in from.

"Did you get lost?" Jack asked pleasantly, stepping back from a corral fence he was working on.

"I went farther'n I aimed to," Red said. "I was thinking about some things."

"You better think a long time," Jack said, "because you got a long time ahead of you to be married in."

"What?" Red said. He thought at first Jack had found out some way about Mary Dove.

"I reckon the things you'as thinking about was mostly Lizzie Munden," Jack said.

Red took a long breath before he answered. "I've thought some about Lizzie," he said.

"She's thought some about you, too, I guess," Jack said. "You can get her if you want her, I expect, but like I said you got a long time to be married."

"I ain't rushing into anything," Red said. "What about you?"

"I ain't studying about getting married a-tall," Jack said.

"Somebody else might be, though."

"I know when I'm well off. And as for Miss Sallie, well I been there before. But this is the first time I ever seen you really get struck on a girl–it's your kind that's got to be careful."

"Do you think I ought to stay away from the meeting tonight?" Red asked.

That was Saturday, the day people were supposed to arrive for the camp meeting at Mr. Johnson's spring. Ralph Edwards the storekeeper had sent word that as many as half a dozen families might be coming to camp, and he himself would try to come and hear the preaching when he could.

Red and Jack had gone earlier in the week to help build the brush arbor: "You boys is getting to be a regular part of the settlement," Mrs. Munden declared.

"You better go," Jack said now. "You're practically a deacon."

"I ain't even a church member," Red said.

"You will be," Jack said. "But I won't, you see, and that's the difference."

Red thought he did see, but it was a very complicated difference having no bearing on himself as the prospective father of a black bastard or Jack as the teller of tales (true or not) about the laying of women.

"We might as well start getting ready," Red said.

It was full summertime in West Texas–fresh, early summer, when the nesting birds still sang, red and yellow flowers bloomed, and grass on the hillsides had not yet turned brown.

Towards sundown, Red and Jack rode to the campground on Mr. Johnson's place, keeping to the high ground, up against the clear, paling sky that arched as it had always done over a vast and empty-looking land.

"I wish it was still as empty as it looks," Red said to himself, and yet felt something in him quickening with anticipation as they neared the meeting site.

"Looky there," Jack said presently, as they topped a gently sloping rise.

From it they looked down on the spring that started the little creek that ran through Mr. Johnson's place. Here the hills did not rise so abruptly as the ones above Mary Dove's spring, nor was there any sign of high rock bluffs like the one that sheltered Mary Dove's pool. From where the men paused, they could see a pool (or hole, as they called it) several hundred yards below the spring; it was larger than Mary Dove's pool, as well as more open and accessible to the surrounding country. Mr. Johnson's sheep were watering there now, muddying the water and messing up the banks, while they baaed incessantly.

Between them and the spring, on either side of the narrow creek, where the land was grassy and nearly level, some half a dozen wagons were scattered, two or three of them still covered with the canvas that sheltered families on their way west. Smoke rose from little separate campfires, where women were frying meat and baking biscuits. Children ran and shouted; several men were squatted together close to the creek, nodding and gesturing in earnest conversation.

Just above the spring stood the Johnsons' small box house, and not far from it the brush arbor, built square and solid looking, its supporting columns hauled from over in the breaks where trees grew sturdier and taller. There was a look about it that, if not permanent, at least promised permanence. Red could almost see it changing to a white frame church house before his very eyes.

"It's hard to believe, ain't it?" he said to Jack, with a sweep of his hand that took in the whole scene.

"Civilization's done caught up with us," Jack said.

"I don't know whether I'm glad to see it or not," Red said.

Jack didn't say whether he was glad—he was moving on towards it already.

By the time the boys were tying their horses among some small hackberries back away from the wagons, the younger Mundens were upon them with cries of greeting and invitations to the evening meal. Sallie and Lizzie walked slowly and sedately in their direction.

All the women were sending children to gather up their menfolk.

"It's suppertime," Lizzie told Red as they met. "I hope you all ain't eat?"

"Every family's fixing their own supper tonight," Sallie explained. "Tomorrow we're all gonna spread dinner together, and you all had better come back then, because me and Lizzie's cooked cake and pie."

"I never expected such pretty girls would be good cooks too," said Jack with practiced ease.

"Wait till you taste what we cooked to start that," Sallie said.

Red chuckled. "That was coming to you, Jack," he said.

Mr. and Mrs. Munden came heartily greeting them now.

"Find you a place to set," Mrs. Munden said, "and the girls'll fill your plates for you."

After they were seated and everyone was fed, she kept looking around her saying, "Ain't this fine? Ain't this just like home?" It was hard to tell when Mrs. Munden ate anything herself, so busy was she urging everyone else to eat and at the same time demanding appreciation of the camp meeting. "Eat all you want," she said—"Red, don't you want some more fried taters?"—but added, "We can't set over supper though, because Brother Michael's gonna start the preaching at sundown and us womenfolks has got to have time to get the dishes washed."

After supper Mr. Munden said, "Come and get acquainted with some of the folks, before preaching time."

But before they had met any of the new people, Mark Johnson appeared saying, "You fellers ain't seen my new boy yet."

This was Mrs. Johnson's first outing with the baby. She sat on a low stool near the Johnson wagon, cradling him in her arms. She had just finished nursing the baby, and as she saw the men approaching she buttoned her dress over deep, full breasts.

Red just glimpsed them, white as the milk the baby sucked. Women were not ashamed, at such a time, if a man saw no more than Red had seen, but he felt disturbed by it. He went and bent awkwardly over the baby, hesitantly touched his pale peach-fuzz hair. The baby, falling asleep, opened unfocused blue eyes for a moment.

"He's shore a baldy, ain't he Red?" said Dora Johnson.

Red could read what she meant by that in her tender eyes and gentle smile: she didn't believe there could be a finer baby boy ever born on the face of the earth.

The older children were crowding around, wanting to take some credit. "What do you think about our baby, Red?" the oldest boy said.

They were all waiting for his answer, looking to him as if the baby's future depended on it: the children gathered close, the mother with her softly lit face just lifted from the rosy infant in her arms, Mark standing right behind her, grinning like a possum.

Red couldn't stand what that scene predicted. "He's a fine young man," he managed to say, and abruptly walked away.

There were so many others coming around now, as suppers were cleared away and the members of the meeting moved about, that Red guessed the family wouldn't even know he had gone. Dora Johnson sat on her stool like a queen on a throne, expecting tribute from everyone, and getting it because it was her due.

Red put it all behind him as rapidly as he could. Jack and Mr. Munden might be staring after him, but he didn't think they would chase him down. After a minute or two, though, he knew someone was following him–presently, he could see the shadow, long and thin along the sun-gilded grass, moving close to his own. He saw by the shape of the head that it was Brother Michael with his sticking-out hair. If the preacher was coming after him, he thought, then he might as well turn and wait.

"I see you share my idea," said Brother Michael, "that a little walk after the evening meal is good for a person."

"Well, you know, Brother Michael–after dinner rest awhile, after supper walk a mile."

"Yes, I've heard that," the preacher said. "And believe it, as I say–good for the soul as well as the body, is what I believe."

"I don't know much about souls," Red said.

"Nor does any man," said the preacher. "What I'm thinking of is the walks I take sometimes, to sort out my thoughts, and maybe say some silent prayers. But for that anybody has to be alone, with plenty of time to spare; I guess you didn't aim to take that kind of a walk."

"No, I'as really just coming down here to look at Mr. Johnson's sheep," Red said. They stopped near the watering hole, where a remnant of the flock was still drinking.

"Of course," said Brother Michael. "You probably wouldn't have much need for the kind of thing I mean. But I've taken a few walks since I've been in this country that seem to bring me closer to God than I have ever been. It's the emptiness, I suppose–the feeling that what God created hasn't yet been spoiled by man. I've never been any place before where you could go so far without seeing any sign of the human race."

"Where've you been walking to, Brother Michael?" Red asked in a way that he hoped sounded unconcerned.

The preacher gestured northward. "I like the creeks and hills," he said.

"And you ain't seen no sign of nobody, I reckon."

"No, did you think I might?"

"No sir—only there's always a chance that you'll run across some squatter."

"I forget you boys must be used to riding over that empty country. You get the same feeling I do walking, maybe."

"I don't know," Red said.

"It's not really a thing to talk of, I guess," the preacher said. "Tell me—what does a cowboy think of all these noisy, crowding sheep?"

"I was wondering if I'd ever make a sheep man," Red truthfully said.

"Why do you reckon Jesus Christ sometimes spoke of the people that followed him as sheep?"

"I don't know," Red said, "unless it's because people is just about as silly."

Brother Michael laughed. "That may be it," he said. "Do you know what the word pastor means?"

"Why preacher, I reckon."

"It does—anyway, a preacher that's in charge of a congregation. But it means sheepherder, too."

"Because the preacher's got to keep his congregation from going astray?"

"Something like that," Brother Michael said. "You know, Red, if I had you in my congregation—if I had a congregation—I would be coming to you to ask what is troubling you."

Red looked up quickly, then down again. He hoped he wasn't blushing. He didn't try to answer.

"Couldn't you tell me, let me help?"

Red shook his head.

"Red, are you a Christian?"

"I'as raised to be. I ain't been baptized."

"Then we'll pray this may be the time. I expect Lizzie Munden may be praying for that, too."

"Lizzie?"

"I've seen your attentions to her. So has everybody else. Nobody–not even Sallie herself–expects Jack Ryan to settle down; but we're all hoping to see you part of the settlement. If the Lord lets us start a church, I can't think of anything better than a young man like you to help build it, with a woman like Lizzie sharing his labors."

The preacher was offering a vision that was either a temptation of the devil (take it, Red–take what they want to give you, desert your wife and fool the folks) or a Christian way of life that he could still, repenting, choose. God alone knew which it was–or maybe the preacher, if Red had the nerve to ask him.

"Well, you'll work things out, I know," Brother Michael said, as Red did not respond. "But if I can ever help you–"

"Much obliged," Red managed to say.

The sun was about to drop behind the little hill above the spring. They walked towards it, the preacher taking great eager strides.

As they reached the camp area where people were nearly ready to go to their meeting place, he said to Red, "I'll go ahead and be ready. You might like other company the rest of the way."

Red found himself at Lizzie's side, or her at his. He saw she was looking after Brother Michael, but she made no comment on what she might have seen.

People had put wagon seats and benches under the arbor, setting them up so as to form a center aisle; and, just as though they were in their old meeting houses back home, they took their proper places–men and big boys on one side, women and girls and little children on the other. Jack was already sitting on the back bench, and Red moved in beside him.

"Getting a little courting done?" Jack whispered.

Red, seeing every head turned toward him as though waiting for the answer, pretended not to hear and did not speak.

The preacher preached by dim lantern light, but he knew his texts by heart. "What came ye into the wilderness to find?" was the beginning of that first sermon of the camp meeting. If it was sin, the preacher said, then you would surely find it; but if you thought to escape there from the just wrath of God, you would be disappointed. "For though you wander so far back among these rocky hills that you reach a place yet untouched by the foot of man, still God is there before you."

Red nearly believed the preacher was looking right into his soul, nearly believed he could find the strength to ask him: "Was it really God I found waiting there? Or was I fooling myself all the time?"

"Repent, repent!" Brother Michael urged.

"What sin, what sin?" Red longed to ask him.

11

After Red told Mary Dove about the sisters, they never came so clear in her mind again. They had appeared to her in a body, all looking much the same, but now after Red's descriptions they scattered like winged seed in the wind. She could never get them all together in her mind again, nor could she quite hold any one of them still long enough to see how she would really be.

But Red knew them all–one from another–how they looked and how they laughed and the kinds of things they talked about. Though he at first seemed not to have noticed or thought about them much, the way he answered Mary Dove's questions told her he had paid attention to them all and taken pleasure in their company.

And so it would be–so of course it would be. She had known that all the time. Some lines of a song came to her–the old story of the girl named Mohee.

Now I am safe landed on my own native shore,
With friends and relations around me once more.

That was how Red was. That was why he had seemed, once he began talking of the Munden girls, so strangely happy and free—so different from the way he had been with Mary Dove since he got the news that his partner was coming.

Friends and relations. The Mundens were not really relations she knew, yet seemed to be: seemed the same as his sisters as she thought of them—were sisters and friends and lovers, too, maybe. Red could love a Munden girl and take her for his wife with the whole world looking on.

Mary Dove rejected the rest of that song.

I look all around me, not one do I see
Who is worthy to compare with the maid of Mohee.

With Red that might not be true. Though he loved her—she never did doubt that he loved her—Mary Dove knew she herself didn't compare with a girl that could stand by his side anywhere, and be the mother of children he would never have to hide.

So I'll turn my course backward, far o'er the blue sea
And spend the rest of my days with the little Mohee.

But would Red, if he had the chance? If he could turn his course backward, would he marry Mary Dove?

Though he loved her, would he? Mary Dove tried to think about that. It was in her mind somehow that it was something she needed to think about. There was some persisting reason, not just the sisters. Really, she had kept the sisters in her mind to block the other out. Only she couldn't any longer.

On his visit they had gone into the dugout, taking his bed back down there. ("Not out here under the arbor," he said. "I know there ain't nobody here, but I can't keep from thinking we ought to be out of sight.") They came together as they had done so many times before, and no matter how many times it was, Mary Dove found herself always with caught breath at the beginning, like a child expecting some wonderful surprise. They came together, and he played his part, but all the same he held something back. The surprise did not quite happen.

If she had tried to tell him how she felt (which she wouldn't do, but if there had been any reason to), she wouldn't have known what to say. She had no words for it now, only a sense of some need not filled–only a kind of coldness yet, as though (but this was not possible) he had not let his body come quite yielding against hers, had somehow kept his own warm strength from going into her as it had always done before.

And still it could be the sisters that caused that difference. Or something else–something to do with sin or wrongdoing. That was in his mind, she knew, but he hadn't told her much about why. In the beginning he had thought it would be wrong for them to marry; but that thought had vanished, or at least never let its presence be known, unless it was that–thin as spider web, strong as silk–that lay between them yesterday.

If it wasn't the sisters, it might have been the preacher that brought that thought back to Red's mind. He might talk of a kind of wrong (a sin) that would worry Red, but she herself didn't believe for a minute they had broken any law of God. Still, something was wrong. Something felt wrong. It might even be wrong of her doing. Somehow.

How strangely times from earliest childhood would now and then come back to her. It was no use to her, trying to think, for she didn't know enough to think. Scolding, she told herself that, and determined to put all the worrisome notions out of her mind. She held the guitar against her (encircled the guitar and the unborn child in her arms), strummed it wondering if any song would come.

What came was a scene so clear it stilled her fingers on the guitar strings, hushed any song she might have sung. So clear and close it came that she could feel the damp warmth of the dugout, see flickering fire shadows on walls dark and dimly red. But just in front of the fire, in a bright circle lit by the flames, was the object most clearly revealed: a baby rabbit, hunched and frightened, just brought in by her father from a nest he had accidentally disturbed with his plow. She stood looking down at it, at the browns like different kinds of fallen winter leaves come together in its fur. "Now be careful, don't squeeze it," her father's words came, as she stooped to take the little tiny scared thing in her two cupped hands.

Oh she never meant to squeeze it, but it was so soft, so warm–she loved it so. She held it to her breast, let her face fall against it, and loved it so much. She knew the moment the life went out of it.

After that she never held a baby rabbit close. Sometimes there would be one (like Rab, last year) left helpless, needing her. But she would be so careful, and always when the time came she would let him go free. Often the rabbit would stay near, as Rab had done, and come to her to be petted and fed, but she never tried to keep one caged or penned.

All that came like a flash to her–a light showing what she must do about Red. She knew how she could do it, and she wouldn't wait, either, for no telling when he would come to her again. She would go to Badger Creek, taking care and being watchful, and she would wait until there was some way to talk to him alone. And she would tell him–a lie; for sometimes (his words well remembered) "a lie is the only thing that will do."

12

Red and Jack did not try to get back to the camp meeting for Sunday morning preaching. They had told the Mundens they wouldn't, for even on Sunday there was work that they couldn't let go.

"Come for dinner, though," the girls and Mrs. Munden insisted, and they accepted that invitation, Jack saying he wouldn't miss that pie and cake if he could help it.

They rode up to the campground just as the people were coming away from the brush arbor. The men were nearly all wearing coats today, and the women had on white or light-colored dresses.

"It looks like a regular Sunday meeting," Red said.

"Look at the preacher," Jack said.

Brother Michael came out of the shadows shining so bright it nearly hurt your eyes to look at him. He had on a pure white suit–nothing black about him but his narrow tie and his shining shoes.

"I wonder what *he* come into the wilderness to find," Jack said.

"The Lord called him. You heard him say that."

"Good enough, I guess," Jack said. "Look, there's Sallie and Lizzie."

They were both wearing pink, and walking together under a parasol. Jack and Red went to meet them. Jack said, "Lizzie looks better than Sallie today; pink's the right color for her."

The girls came smiling, offering "Howdy do's."

"We're fixing to help put out dinner now," Lizzie said, "but if you boys will find a good grassy place to set we'll bring your plates in a little while."

"We want to be sure you sample our cooking," Sallie said.

The boys had time to greet the preacher and some other acquaintances before Mrs. Munden rang the school bell she had with her for calling meals. Everybody came together and listened to Brother Michael ask the blessing, and then Red and Jack found a place to wait for their dinner to be served.

The couples sat just enough apart to carry on their separate conversations during the meal.

"Now what kind of cake have you made?" Red asked Lizzie.

"It's a jelly layer cake," she said.

"Did you make the jelly too?"

"Oh yes–we brought it from home; it's blackberry."

"My favorite," Red said.

"I guess there's not any blackberries out here."

"Nothing but sour plums and algerita berries."

"Do they make jelly out of them berries?" Lizzie asked.

"Some folks do," Red said. "They're better'n nothing."

"When do they get ripe?"

"They're ripe now. I think I saw a bush over yonder a little piece when me and Jack rode in. We'll go look at it after dinner if you want to."

"We might do that," Lizzie said. "We'll have a hour or so before preaching starts."

As people finished eating, they began to mill around. The girls had to help clean up and wash dishes, and by the time Lizzie came to Red again he had lost sight of Jack.

"Reckon we ought to get Jack and Sallie to go with us?" Red said.

"I don't see 'em anywhere," said Lizzie.

"Let's don't look for 'em then," Red said.

"She's gone off with the parasol, I guess."

"You won't need it for just that little walk."

"I like to keep white though. I'll get my bonnet."

He had scarcely noticed before how very fair she was, how smooth and soft her skin. He had forgotten how hard girls tried to keep that way.

"We oughtn't to go off this way," Lizzie said as she came back wearing her ruffled Sunday bonnet.

"It ain't far–just over that first little rise."

So they went, and came to the algerita berry bush growing on the sloping side of a shallow little draw that drained into the main creek. He led her to the low grayish shrub and reached out to pick a berry.

"You got to be awful careful of them stickery leaves," he said. "Let me pick you some to taste."

He offered a few in the palm of his hand, and she tasted.

"They've got a whang," she said. "I don't know whether I like 'em or not."

"They make fairly good jelly," he said.

"I'll try another one," she said, reaching. Then she drew quickly back. "Oh, I've stuck one of them leaves in my hand."

She lifted a hand, with a scratch across the back of it that was bleeding a little. The blood was redder than the berries and the hand was paper white.

"Do you think it looks bad, Red?" Lizzie asked.

He thought, Lord, how long have I been standing here staring at her hand? His eyes were fixed upon it. With some thought of redeeming himself (or with no thought at all–later on, he couldn't be sure) he took the hand in both of his and raised it to his lips and kissed it–kissed the blood away.

"Red!" she gasped.

"I done it without thinking," he said. "I apologize." He was still holding her hand, still seeing how slender, soft, and white it was.

She drew it away. "It's all right," she said. "But you surprised me."

"Does it hurt any more?" he asked.

"Not hardly a-tall," she said.

She stood unmoving and very pale–not from scratching her hand, he guessed. They didn't say anything. She would scream and run, he thought, if she knew what was in his mind: the puzzle of what that pale stillness concealed. He caught some hint of a deep feeling in her, but not (surely not, but he wondered) the sort of passion that formed so natural a part of Mary Dove. A decent woman–a woman raised right, Lizzie Munden, his married sisters–went quietly to bed in the dark and beneath the covers let their husbands take the pleasure that belonged to them. Or so he had always believed. Now he was wondering two things: was that true, and if so (should something undreamed of happen, and he ever come to marry that kind of woman) could a decent woman ever be enough for him?

"Red, what's wrong with you?" Lizzie asked at last.

"I was thinking about some things I couldn't tell you," he said. "We'd better go now."

She took his hand and held it for an instant, as if to say she understood. He wondered how close she could come, with her guessing.

People were gathering at the arbor when they came back in sight of the camp, and they separated to join their proper groups.

At the beginning of this meeting Brother Michael announced that already there were five people ready for baptism—a young married couple that had asked, the night before, to be prayed for, and three children who, having reached the age of accountability, were ready to be Christians.

"Glory hallelujah!" came several shouts.

"Yes, brothers and sisters," the preacher responded. "The Lord is blessing us."

What they all wanted now, the preacher and his congregation, was more sinners coming forth to be saved. Red could hear starched skirts rustling and feet moving on the ground as the listeners settled back in anticipation.

Now in the cool dimness, under the sound of the preacher's exhorting voice, Red felt the perplexities and the longing of the night before come back to him. Anguished, he silently prayed that a way to live a Christian life, and still bring no one pain, might be made plain to him. Perhaps he was not wholly silent; Jack, sitting beside him, turned sharply once and looked at him.

No longer comprehending the sense of the words, but only the rise and fall of Brother Michael's threats and promises, Red did not notice when the sermon was over. Vaguely aware that the congregation was standing, he stood too and joined in the song that was an invitation to lost souls: "Come ye sinners, poor and needy."

And that was Mary Dove's song. Red stood and sang with

the rest, but when they came to the chorus about ten thousand charms he couldn't go on.

"Oh Lord," he groaned, and at first didn't know he had spoken aloud.

There was only one thing to do, as the singing sank low and all eyes turned upon him. He stumbled up the grassy aisle and went on his knees in front of Brother Michael. "Pray for me," he cried hoarsely, and hid his face in his hands.

Several people came to him when the service was over, shaking his hand, assuring him of their prayers. Mrs. Munden hugged him. There were tears in her eyes. Most of the women had been crying, but Lizzie was dry-eyed and pale, paler than she had been by the berry bush.

Finally they all went away and left him, as they must, alone with Brother Michael.

The preacher knelt beside him. "What is it, son?" he said. "Can you tell me now?"

"No, I can't tell you," Red said. "I'm a sinner, that's all."

"It's enough," Brother Michael said, "if you repent."

"How can I tell for sure," Red finally asked, "if I repent?"

"So it's that way, is it?" the preacher said.

"It's that way," Red said.

"It might not be as bad as you think," the preacher said, "if you could only tell me."

"I can't tell you," Red said.

"Then we can only pray," said Brother Michael, and they knelt a long time together.

Red felt surprised to see the bright sunshine when they left the brush arbor. He had felt concealed in darkness there, and now all eyes seemed upon him. "I got to go," he said.

"Yes, you would feel that way," Brother Michael said. "But you'll come back."

"If I can, I will," Red said.

"Go and say goodbye to Lizzie," Brother Michael said.

"I can't," Red said.

But Brother Michael was beckoning. "I want you to tell

her," he said. "And she wants to be told, for she is coming."

"Red's going home to be by himself for a while," he said to Lizzie as she came and met them. "We understand that, don't we?"

She looked gravely at Red. "Yes," she said.

"I'll come back when I can," Red said, looking down from her face. "I've got to think."

"Yes, think," she said, "and pray." She seemed about to raise her hands to him. He looked and saw the red mark on one of them. She put them down at her sides again. "I want you to come back," she said, "and oh Red, I'll be so glad for you to be saved."

She turned and walked away, with her tidy little steps, not hurrying.

Red watched her. Everyone was watching her, and he thought, "She done that for me."

But she had a clear conscience, and that made the difference. He couldn't stand all those eyes turned on him.

"Tell Jack I'm gone," he said to Brother Michael. "Tell him I'll see about things at camp, to stay for preaching tonight if he wants to."

"I'll tell him," the preacher said. "You come back soon, Red."

"Thanks," Red muttered, and ran to his horse.

13

Red rode fast awhile, and then very slowly, heading vaguely toward Badger Creek. Sometimes he talked to Sangaree, sometimes to God.

"I don't much care where you go, Sangaree," he said, letting the reins hang loose, "but I guess we'll have to go home some time."

Have to see Jack, hear what they said about Red at the camp meeting. And then would he have to go back there, have to see Lizzie, have to tell her "Sorry, you'as rejoicing a little too soon"?

"Oh God, why did you let me do that?" he cried aloud. He didn't know whether he meant his unChristian wedding with Mary Dove, his misunderstood friendship with Lizzie, or the fool he had made of himself at the meeting. Or he guessed he really did need praying for; he hoped the prayers did some good.

Letting Sangaree choose the way, he found they were drifting eastward, a way that could lead to Mary Dove's dugout. He jerked the reins sharply: "Not there," he said. "Not till I've got things figured out better."

As he approached the camp he reckoned the sun was about two hours high. Mrs. Munden, he thought, would be telling the girls what to set out for supper. Sallie would be hunting out good things for Jack's plate. And Lizzie–he wondered if Lizzie would feel lonesome.

He had just started down the slope into the little creek valley where the dugout camp was located when he heard someone calling his name. It was a woman's voice, or a girl's. Someone must have come after him from the meeting was the first thing he thought. No, something must be wrong with Mary Dove. After the first wild moment he knew it was Mary Dove's voice–but if she had hurt herself some way, if she'd had a miscarriage, she couldn't be there, calling him.

She was walking towards him, from down the creek. She seemed all right, but it would be no ordinary thing bringing her here.

He hurried to meet her. "What in the world is the matter?" he demanded as they came close together. He reined in his horse.

"Oh Red, I've been waiting so long," she said. "I thought I wouldn't see you."

"What's the matter?" he repeated, dismounting and hurrying to her side.

"Ain't nothing the matter," she said, "but I had to see you."

"Ain't nothing the matter," he cried, "and you come here! I thought you'd know better than that." It was a relief to get mad at her.

"I was careful, Red, really I was. I know how to keep hid, and I come so slow and watchful. There wasn't nobody here, and I hid to wait. I thought I could find some way to see you by yourself, and keep out of sight. But I waited so long, and I started home, but still looking back sometimes. And at last I seen you a-coming."

"Well, what is it then?"

"I can't tell you in a word or two, I need to talk to you."

"Well, let's get you home. I don't look for Jack till after dark, but you can't tell what may happen. Do you want to ride behind?"

"I'd rather walk than ride."

"I'll walk along with you, and lead Sangaree. You can tell me whatever it is as we go."

Mary Dove had never deliberately made up a lie to tell before. She remembered how sometimes when she was a little girl she had slipped into quick little saving lies, and her father said, "You mustn't tell me stories, Mary Dove." "I never meant to, Papa," she had said to that, and he said, "Mostly people tells lies because they're scared, and I don't want you to be scared of me, ever. My papa used to whip me sometimes till the blood run, and I would lie to him to keep from getting hurt–but even lying that way was wrong, and I wish now I hadn't done it. If a boy's taught right he'll take a whipping before he'll lie–and so would a girl, if she had to."

Mary Dove's father never had whipped her; yet sometimes she would cry if he only seemed displeased with something she had done. And so it was, when she was very young, that she told some little story now and then; but never in her life before had she given time and thought, deliberately, to the making of a lie.

"Well, what is it?" Red said, after they had walked awhile in silence.

She had made the lie, but didn't know yet the best way to tell it.

"Well?" Red said again.

She guessed there was only one way. "Red, you have got to leave me," she said.

But that was what he was going to tell her. Or might, when he thought things out. After he repented. After he was baptized, and could see more clearly what the right thing was to do.

"We done wrong, Red," she went on. "I reckon you thought it all the time, and now I know it too—we broke the law of God."

That was the real and necessary lie that she had determined to tell. Nothing else would have been enough. She might have said, "I've been wrong, done wrong, keeping you away from your friends and relations," and he might have said (even lying might have said), "No, Mary Dove, for I love you more than them."

"We stood before God and made our promises," he said. "I thought you believed that was right for us."

"I did at first. But it wasn't. We done wrong, and you believe that yourself. Since you been hearing that preacher you believe it. I know you do."

"Do you think me leaving you would make things right again?"

"You *said* there was something folks could do when they had broke God's law."

"I said repent."

"Ain't it repenting to quit doing the wrong thing?"

"Not exactly."

"You said you'd tell me about sin and repenting and all. Tell me now, so I'll understand it."

"It ain't easy to tell."

Mary Dove waited, not saying anything. They were going slowly along, among rocks and bushes on the bank of the creek; would follow it a piece, staying out of sight of anyone who might come over the hills from the campground.

It wasn't easy to tell. In Red's mind the threat of hell was as real as flames in a fireplace, and the reasons for staying out of the fire were sensible and clear. But he wasn't any preacher. He sought words carefully and slowly, as he found safe steps to take.

"I don't hardly know where to start," he said. With Mary Dove you never could start far enough back. "We never did exactly talk about it, but I reckon you know what happens to folks when they die."

"I've thought about that. I reckon there's part of them that goes to be with God. I guess it's what the song means about rising and going to Jesus."

"That's right," he said, "–to Heaven. But some will go to hell."

"That's where the devil is."

"And it's where folks will go when they die, if they haven't repented of their sins and joined the church and all."

"I guess if they don't know about God, and try to go by his laws, they don't get to be with him when they die. And Jesus don't take 'em in his arms."

"It ain't just like that, exactly. It's worse than just not being with God."

"Could it be?"

"It shore could. If you was to burn in the hottest kind of fire you can imagine, forever and ever, not ever ending, wouldn't that be worse?"

"How could that happen, Red?"

"I don't know, but it could. The Bible says so, and the preacher says so."

"Is that what happens to you if you break God's laws?"

"Unless you repent. And I got to try to tell you what that is. See, I could leave you, like you said I ought to do. But if I still thought about you and wanted you, and was sorry I left you, that wouldn't be repenting. I'd have to be sorry I ever loved you in the first place."

"I didn't know it was so hard," said Mary Dove.

"It's hard. It's the hardest part, and then you got to be baptized–that means the preacher ducks you under the water to wash your sins away–and then you're ready to join the church–in the name of the Lord Jesus Christ."

"Could I join the church, Red?"

"Why not?"

"Can niggers?"

"Some places they can, I reckon. Course they can–they've got nigger churches, in towns and all."

"If they don't live where there's nigger churches, do they go to hell?"

"Oh I don't know. How would I know? You're always trying to mix me up, Mary Dove."

"I ain't, Red. There's just so much I don't understand."

"Well, I don't understand it all either, and I ain't pretending I do. But of course we have sinned–you're right about that."

"Maybe God won't blame you–I talked you into doing what we done."

"I'm more to blame than you, for I knowed better."

"I was disobeying Papa when I took you in."

"But you never understood what it was we'as getting into. I ought to have kept us from sinning, because I'd been taught Christian ways."

"What is the sin, Red–us being together without the right kind of marrying, or me being part nigger? Which is the worst?"

They were on the hills now, crossing from Badger Creek into the area where the little draws ran into Spring Creek. The sun was low and red.

"Out here," Red said, "it don't seem like it could matter either way. It seems like it's just you and me and God, and we ain't hurting nothing, only loving each other. And then I look at you, and I can see easy now that there's a baby on the way. And I think what will become of him—he's got to live in the world, and there's people coming in all around us and he'll have to grow up among them. And I know I can't keep you away from them much longer."

"And you can't live the way you really want to live," said Mary Dove.

He looked at her wonderingly. "Is that the reason?" he asked.

"The reason for what?"

"For telling me to leave you."

"Oh." She caught her breath. Maybe, after all, she wasn't any good at lying, but she said, "No. Or I guess it's part of the reason. Part of why the thing we done is sin."

"Yes," he said. "It's pretty complicated. I been knowing that a long time."

"So you've got to leave me."

"And what if I did? Now I ain't agreeing to nothing—but say we do try to repent, and of course you're right in a way. Separating might not prove we repented, but we shore enough couldn't go on living together and try to pretend that we was sorry of our sin. Say we did separate—maybe I could live like you think I want to, but just how would you live? I don't reckon you think I'm going off and leave you out here by yourself with a baby on the way."

"I've thought of all that. At first I thought it would be harder for me now than it was when I found out Papa wouldn't come back and I had to try to live by myself. But except for missing you, Red, it won't be. 'Cause I know now why Papa kept me away from folks—I know who I am now—and I reckon if I don't try to pretend nothing or break any laws I can go to town now the same as anybody and buy what I need at a store. I reckon niggers can buy things, if they got the money."

"Don't talk silly. Where you aiming to get money?"

"Just like Papa did. I can raise sheep, and other things.

And pretty soon I'll have some help, and won't need to be lonesome. I guess I can have a baby and take care of it by myself; I've got as much sense as the cows and the sheep and the wild animals. I don't even know whether it's natural for the papa to have anything to do with raising the baby or not."

"Don't talk silly, I told you. Whatever happens to us, I'll take care of you. I may be a sinner, but I ain't that sorry."

"I know you could help me some at first. I thought maybe you could help me get some land around the dugout. Looks like I could get it the same way you'as talking about getting it from the state."

"I don't know. You might."

"Well, you could see. You could help me get started. I'll soon have a nice little herd of sheep, and I aim to keep plenty of chickens on hand. I thought if you could get me a cow or two I might keep a little bunch of cows, and then I could always have meat and milk."

He had pictured her breaking into helpless tears if he ever hinted he might leave her–he ought to have known Mary Dove wouldn't do the thing he expected her to do. She could get him so mixed-up: now he seemed to have his feelings hurt because she was offering him what might turn out to be the answer to his prayers and the prayers of the whole congregation. They might be praying for him at meeting now, this very minute, and he would soon be free. Would be saved, and free.

And Mary Dove doing just fine without him.

"I don't know," he said. "I ain't agreeing to nothing yet."

"I have made up my mind," she said.

They had come to the dugout. She went and sat on the arbor bench.

"I'm pretty tired," she said.

He sat beside her. "I'd better get right on back," he said.

"Yes," she said.

He put his arms around her, leaned close to her face.

"Don't kiss me, Red," she said.

He sat away from her. "Not even that?" he asked.

even that," she said. "You might as well go on."

go then," he said. "But I'll be back and see you in a r two, because we ain't decided nothing yet."

Goodbye, Red."

He said goodbye. He went and mounted Sangaree and rode homeward. The sun was setting clear, a little north of the way he took. South of there, on another creek, preaching would be starting.

14

While Red was riding to Badger Creek the moon rose, nearly full. Later, waiting for Jack to come in, he sat on the little hill above their camp and looked out over the world around him, which, though familiar and clear in the moonlight, was yet transformed, with all the warmth and color gone from it.

He could hear owls and coyotes, but their voices were thinned by distance. The reality of everything seemed to be slipping away from him, leaving just the shadow of the world he had known. He had meant to try to think: what to do about Mary Dove, how to reclaim his own soul, whether any ordinary life with any ordinary woman (Lizzie Munden) ever could be his. It was easier to let it all go.

He nearly forgot Jack was coming. Then the thud of a horse's hoofs and a shouted hello began to bring the world close around him again. Jack could see him up there against the light sky. He might as well go down into the circle of lantern light and say "Shore I'm all right. How did things go at the meeting?"

He was able to do that. Jack was a good old boy: he didn't say much about the show Red put on.

"Why they're really shouting hallelujah tonight," he said. "They got three more sure converts, and they're talking pretty serious about organizing a church before they break up."

"When they gonna break up?"

"Well, they ain't decided that yet. But folks is beginning to talk about needing to get home and get to work, you know. I tell you the truth: I think they're holding out for you."

"Me."

"Shore. You oughta heard the praying and seen them womenfolks a-bawling for you. I tell you one thing: if you don't come across now, you just as well never figure on going amongst them Munden gals no more."

"I'll be a hardened sinner in their eyes."

"Course you will. In your own too, I reckon, and that's the main thing. I don't know why you don't go back over there and say whatever it is you got to say and get yourself baptized and join that church."

"No, you don't know."

"I can guess. You got some crazy idea in your head that there's something you done so bad you can't afford to. That preacher harping on repenting all the time. But Lord, Red, if you ain't repenting all over the place I don't know what you'd call it. Repenting means being sorry of your sins, as I understand it, and you're about the sorriest looking feller lately that I ever did see."

"You may be right."

"I am. You go join that church."

Red lay awake that night trying to pray. When daylight came he had one new thought: once he was baptized, the Lord might let him see more clearly what way he ought to go. He made up his mind to be guided by that thought.

The next night Red and Jack rode into the camp meeting just at sundown. "I don't want to talk to nobody till it's over," Red said.

He sat through the sermon without hearing anything Brother Michael said, and when the invitation was issued (the preacher standing before the congregation with outstretched arms), he rose and went like a sleepwalker to kneel and accept it.

/ hallelujah!" he heard Mrs. Munden cry. "The lost ...1."

...r the service, when the general rejoicing had subsided, ... came to him quietly, with shining face and eyes. "After th... baptizing," Red whispered to her, "we'll talk about some things."

Most of the congregation stayed together awhile in earnest conversation. It was time to end the meeting and go home, all agreed. If they had the baptizing the next day, with the closing service in the brush arbor afterward, they would have done all they ever hoped to do.

The subject of the new church arose. They would meet there under the arbor awhile, no doubt, but where would be the best place to build the church house?

"What we had better decide first," Mrs. Munden said, lifting her voice above the rest, "is where we will have the baptizing."

"Well, I thought down here on my creek," Mr. Johnson said.

"Them sheep has got it awful messy, Papa," Mrs. Johnson said.

Brother Michael now stood before them. "I know of a place," he said. "You know I have walked sometimes over the hills and down these little valleys, seeking to commune with the Lord. I came one day, going along a little creek not more than two or three miles from here, to a pretty little round pool with a clean rock shore sloping down gently into the water. I have never seen anything just like it in this country–or indeed anywhere. It's like a little jewel set down among green grass and trees, with hills rising around it and a rock bluff, so that herds of animals would find it hard to water there. I took it that day as a sign: the Lord would bless my work and, therefore, I would come there bringing for baptism the first fruits of my harvest for the Lord."

"Amen, amen," and "His will be done," some immediately called. Others were asking, "Now just how far is it?" and "Can we get close to it in the wagon?"

The cries and questions went around and around R
head like humming flies that he wasn't allowed to slap at. H
could think of no protest to make. He knew what the outcome would be. The congregation would accept Brother Michael's sign from the Lord—the sign that would lead them unerringly to the site of his own secret sin.

And Mary Dove? He could get away in the night and go and warn her, tell her to stay in the dugout with bolted door; but he thought, "They would find her anyway, track her down and have the truth at last." Or it might be they would go to the pool and no farther, never even know a dwelling place stood near. It was in the hands of God now. Red had put it there himself.

"Thy will be done," he said, and Mrs. Munden nodded approvingly upon him.

15

Mary Dove thought Red might come back to her that first day. If he really loves me, he won't be off somewhere figuring things out, was what she truly believed. Though she had sent him away with her mind well made up that she could live without him, when the moon shone down on her still alone that night she said, "I can't fool myself no longer," and she let her heart break.

Next morning she came awake lying in dewy grass on a hillside, and she remembered how she flung herself there after wandering for hours in the moonlight, having grieved past endurance. The sun was up, warming her already, and the sheep had come grazing around her. It was their curious baaing that woke her, she supposed.

"Well, you're still here," she said to them.

She stood up and looked around her. The air was fresh and flowery, clear as a dewdrop. A few small clouds the color of doves' breasts hung in the east. On a day like this she used to

could fly like a bird from hill to hill. She felt a
ging in her breast.

not gone either," she said.

she could live without Red. She might have fooled
ut how easy it would be, but this morning again she believed she could do it. She thought she would go to the pool when the morning work was done.

Baptizing, she thought. After Red had explained to her how the preacher would wash away sins and make a person ready for God, she had wondered if the old way she had of reaching God was a sort of baptizing.

"In the name of the Lord Jesus Christ," was what the preacher would say. "I don't know Jesus," Mary Dove said to herself, "but God knows I can't help it and may come anyway."

So thinking, she followed the little clear-running creek to the pool where now willows and cottonwoods had turned pure summer green. On an overhanging branch a dove, as always, nested. Her mate perched nearby and falsely mourned.

"Mourn for me," said Mary Dove.

She had taken to wearing her old white shifts again. They were more comfortable than her mother's close fitting dresses, and the sheep and cows and chickens liked them just as well.

She undressed now and unbound her hair, then sat awhile in the sun with her feet in the water.

"Mourn for me, dove," she said again.

It became a song.

"Mourn for me.
You dove mourn for everything,
But I will not mourn.
I will be glad, and the birds on their nests
will be glad, and the trees and sweet flowers.
You dove can do all the mourning for us.
And all the rest of the world
Will be glad
And find God."

She plunged into the deep part of the pool. Down in that pale green place she had no thought of blue sky or birds singing. There was just the feel of them in her body, the feel of every good thing filling her, swelling inside her. Swelling like the baby inside her. Almost, she forgot who put that baby there: hadn't it come as naturally as birds nesting or clouds gathering?

She came to the surface, not quite content but nearly so. She thought she would sit in the sun awhile, and then go in again.

As she lifted her head from the water she heard a strange sound. Animals milling–sheep or cattle, was what she thought at first. She shook her head, clearing her ears, keeping herself just afloat, ready to go under the water and out of sight.

For those were people's voices. This certainty had quickly come to her, though without any understanding of how they could be there, or where they could be going, moving along the creek below her, coming closer, louder, all the time.

The dove hushed and flew away. Small birds stopped singing. It seemed to Mary Dove that even the breeze ceased to blow, and the ripples stilled on the surface of the water.

The people were singing, and she could make out the words that they sang:

> *"Shall we gather at the river,*
> *Where bright angel feet have trod?"*

She let herself down to the bottom of the pool. She did not know how long it would take these strangers to go by, but she could reach no other hiding place. If they went on, it might be they never would see her. She stayed as long as she could, then hung just below the surface.

They were not going on. They were standing on the hillside, singing.

Suddenly she heard a loud shout. With her face barely out of the water she heard someone cry, "What is that?" Other cries came: "It's a person! It's a body!"

w with terror, Mary Dove could float quietly no hey had seen her already. They had seen her, and s there to do but try to run away? She clambered out e rock shore, and stood and looked wildly about her.

igger!" came a high piercing scream from the hillside where a host of pale men and women in white shirts and white dresses hovered like terrible strange birds.

They began to move down the hill to the place where the creek bank sloped gently to the pool. Mary Dove looked helplessly to where she had left her dress in the crotch of the cottonwood tree. Terror held her motionless.

"I ain't gonna be baptized where no nigger's been taking a bath," a girl yelled angrily. "I'd go to hell first."

"Look at the shape she's in," a woman cried, "and showing herself bare!"

"Shameless! Shameless!" Many took up that cry.

Mary Dove dared again to look at them coming upon her. But they turned to a blur before her eyes. Red might be there –she didn't know, couldn't see. She tried a step–if only she could run.

"Grab her!" a man shouted. "Don't let her get away till we find out where she come from."

A long time ago Mary Dove had dreamed such terror, but she had never guessed that it could really be. It was, anyhow, the most there could be. The rocks moved under her feet, and blessed blackness came relieving her.

In the same instant Red, released from the shock that had gripped him, saw Mark Johnson step forward reaching out toward Mary Dove; and then the only thing in his mind was to prevent that touch, to save her–from what was no way clear to him, as he ran, thrusting through the people around him, not knowing or caring who anyone was.

Lizzie put her hand on his arm and cried "Red!"–he couldn't have called her by name.

He reached Mary Dove in time to keep her from collapsing on the rock. He picked up the wet shining body in his arms and held it, kissing the mouth, calling Mary Dove back to him. It was long minutes before he remembered that the white-clad crowd (struck still and silent, too) stood looking on.

When he remembered he glanced at them once, then turned away from them to carry Mary Dove home.

16

"I lied to you, Red."

That was the thing that came to her first when she opened her eyes and saw Red's anxious face close to hers. She lay on the bed in the dugout, still naked and damp, with the cover drawn up over her.

"I lied too," he said. "To you, and myself, and the preacher and everybody. But it's all right, we've got things straight now."

"I never did want you to leave me," she said.

"I never will again," he said.

She closed her eyes and lay still and quiet, while he held her hand.

At last he said, "Mary Dove, you're all right, ain't you?"

"Yes, Red."

"I mean, you don't hurt nowhere–you really are all right–you and the baby."

"We're all right," she said.

"You lay still awhile," he said.

He boiled some coffee and took her a cup of it sweetened and weakened with milk. He supported her with his arm and held the cup for her while she slowly drank it.

"I could get up," she said.

"You lay there," he said. "I got a lot of taking care of you to do."

He went to the trunk and took out one of her old shifts. "You want to put this on?" he asked.

"The others is too tight," she said.

"I'll get you some clothes, Mary Dove," he said, "and some baby clothes. You're gonna have what other women do."

"Did you find a way?" she asked him.

"Yes!" he fiercely answered.

He dressed her now as he might a baby, and laid her gently down and pulled the rough sheet over her.

"Rest," he said.

She lay quiet. He sat on the bed beside her, just touching her hand with his.

He thought about the answer he had given her. That was no lie: he had found a way. The only way, he knew now, that he would ever want to live was close to Mary Dove. Where they would live and how he would make a living were details he still had to settle; what he knew for sure was that he would keep her close to him always, and take care of her, and beget her children. He hoped God might call that marriage, but if it was sin then sin would be their way.

Her eyes were closed and her lips were gently smiling. While he sat watching her, wondering if she was really asleep, he heard someone holler outside.

For an instant he pictured Mr. Munden coming with his shotgun (having imagined more than had happened between Lizzie and Red), but he did not think that this was Mr. Munden's voice.

He got up, and Mary Dove's eyes opened questioningly. "It's all right," he said.

He went to the top of the dugout steps and saw Brother Michael standing just outside the shadow of the arbor, still wearing his dazzling white suit. In the full sunshine even his sticking-out hair looked shining and white.

"Come in, Brother Michael," Red called. "It ain't much of a place but we call it home." He meant to leave no doubts now, in anybody's mind.

The preacher came under the arbor then, and Red stepped forth to meet him, holding out his hand.

The preacher took it. "My poor boy," he said.

"You seen how it is," Red said. "If you want to come in you'll be welcome."

"Of course I want to come in," the preacher said.

Red led him down the steps. "My wife," he said, "is laying down, but she feels better now."

"I am glad to know it," the preacher said. He went and stood near where Mary Dove lay, with her hair a dark cloud on the pillow. "And so this is your wife," he said.

"She is," Red said. "Mary Dove," he said, "shake hands with Brother Michael. Brother Michael, this here is my wife, Mary Dove."

She began to rise, but the preacher said, "Please don't get up, Mary Dove," and bent to take her hand.

"Set down, Brother Michael," Red said. "We've got some coffee ready, would you like to have a cup?"

"Thank you," the preacher said. "I would enjoy it."

"I'll just set the pot over the coals a little bit," Red said, "and then I'll have a cup with you."

"I never would have guessed that such a pretty little place as this was around the bend from the pool I found one day," the preacher said. "I never did see such a pretty location for a dugout, or a dugout fixed up so nice. That arbor makes me think of the garden bowers I used to see folks build back in the Old States."

"We think it's nice," said Red.

"But I understood," the preacher said, "that you lived at the camp with your partner."

"Wait just a minute till I get the coffee, Brother Michael," Red said, "and then if you want to listen I'll tell you how it is. I'll tell you what I couldn't tell before, when I tried to repent of my sins, but I'll have to admit that right now the only thing I really know I'm sorry for is ever leaving Mary Dove by herself and going off and acting like I didn't have her."

"You are sorry you misled people, Red?" Brother Michael said softly.

"Yes, I'm sorry for that," Red said.

Red went and looked down at Mary Dove. She was lying still, with her eyes closed again, but he thought she was listening. He poured the coffee into Mary Dove's thick white cups and brought them to the table where the preacher had sat down.

"I'm sorry for that," Red said again. "I'm sorry for a lot of things, but I ain't sorry I've got Mary Dove, and if you want to know now I'll tell you how I come to have her, and be here living with her."

"I want to hear that story," Brother Michael said, "but first I had better tell you that I was sent here by my congregation to deal with you, and to tell you what they have decided."

"I can see they wouldn't want me in their church," Red said, "but I don't know what business they got deciding anything but that."

"They think it's their business," Brother Michael said. "Mr. Munden particularly. It was all I could do to keep him from coming after you with that gun of his."

"I don't see why he'd try to go that far," Red said. "I know they must be mad at me, but I never promised Lizzie nothing."

"You knocked her down, back at the pool, when you went running through the crowd to catch Mary Dove."

"Oh Lord," Red said. "Was she hurt?"

"No, not hurt."

"I guess," Red said, "that what Mr. Munden has decided is if he ever lays eyes on me again he'll kill me."

"He's a Christian, Red," the preacher said. "But still you can see why they don't want you living among them."

"You mean they're gonna run me out of the country," Red said.

"They want you to leave," the preacher said, "but we'll talk more about that later. I want to hear your story."

"It goes back to the spring of last year," Red said.

While he told the tale Mary Dove came and sat on the bench beside him and he held her hand.

"And I have sometimes thought," he added when he had told it all, "that if only you never had come here–if they hadn't had that camp meeting. But no," he broke off, "it all had to happen–we never could have lived the way we hoped we could."

"No, you never could have, Red. Even if nobody ever had come here to settle–even if Jack hadn't come to work with you–you couldn't have done that way. It went against your raising, and you couldn't have been content."

"I was raised to be a Christian," Red said, "and now I guess I can't even get baptized."

"I hoped to baptize you," Brother Michael said.

"But I don't repent," Red said. "I never could repent of loving Mary Dove."

Mary Dove looked up now and spoke for the first time. "Preacher," she said, "is it really a sin, what me and Red done?"

"Don't you think it is, Mary Dove?"

"I don't know," she said. "Sin's new to me. I never even heard the word until Red come."

"There is no one without sin," the preacher said, "but it may be Red brought you the knowledge of it."

"But I can't wish there hadn't been Red," said Mary Dove. "And I don't know for sure that we sinned–we married the only way we could, just like Red told you."

"You deceived yourselves," the preacher said. "You didn't really get married."

"We would've married some other way," said Mary Dove, "but Red said there's a law–"

"There is a law," the preacher said. He looked steadily at the girl who sat before him. "You couldn't get a license in any place I know about, or any preacher that would say the words to link you two in holy matrimony."

"But is it God's law?" asked Mary Dove. "Or is it people's law?"

Brother Michael got up and stood as if about to preach a

sermon. At last he only sighed, and began to walk about the room.

"Can you answer that question, Brother Michael?" Red asked.

"I have never seen the answer written among the words of God," the preacher finally said, "and I cannot say for sure. But I will say this: the people believe you have sinned, for you have spurned their ways, and few of them have ever seen anything as wicked as the scene you two enacted at the baptizing pool. It may be God will look deeper than they can look, will judge as they won't judge and I can't judge. Their judgment is that they cannot tolerate your presence. They have sent word that you must leave here at once, and no matter what my own feeling might be I could not prevent any action they might take against you."

"I don't think I followed everything you said, Brother Michael," Red said. "But I understood that last part. I reckon Mr. Munden ain't the only one that's got a gun."

"Does it mean we've got to leave here, Red?" Mary Dove asked.

"Yes, it means that, Mary Dove."

"I can't even imagine how I would feel anywhere but here," she said. "Everything I ever did know is here. I ain't sure Red believes it, but I found God here. God would come to me in the pool or on the hill at sundown. There was always just some special places I could find God, and I guess there won't be no such places for me now."

The preacher stopped walking, stood beside Mary Dove.

"So you found God," he said.

"You won't believe it either," she said.

"I understand it," he said. "But you can't leave God behind you, Mary Dove."

"Oh I know God is everywhere–in a kind of a way. I won't find him, that's all."

"I preach that people find God through Jesus Christ."

"But me and Red can't find Jesus," she said, "because we

can't get baptized. I could find God by myself, before all these people come and got between us, but you can't get to Jesus that way."

The preacher rose and began to pace the room again.

"You may find a way," the preacher said.

"We've doomed ourselves to hell," Red said.

The preacher walked and talked. "Now son, that may not be so," he said. "I can't tell what God's will for you is, but I have heard there may be places where folks feel different about couples like you and Mary Dove. It's possible you may be married, as you believe, in God's view, and you may find some place where you can marry by the law, be known as man and wife, and go to church together."

"But where is this place, Brother?" Red asked.

"I only know what I have heard men tell. I don't know much about state laws, but go–go west or north, I think, and ask, when you've gone far enough, and pray, and God will guide you where you ought to go."

"Do you believe that, Brother Michael?" Red asked.

"I believe that if you trust in God you'll find a way," the preacher said. "Yes, I think I can promise you that."

"Then this is good news," Mary Dove cried eagerly.

"It may be," Red said. "But the real news is that we've got to leave here soon. We haven't got much time, I guess." He turned to Brother Michael questioningly.

"Tomorrow morning is the time they set."

"I haven't even got my horse," Red said.

"Jack sent your horse and your pack mare," the preacher said, "with your things from the camp. He said he guessed you wouldn't be wanting to see him, but if there was anything he could do to send him word."

"Jack really was my friend."

"He said he'd stay away from the baptizing–we're having that in the morning."

"At my pool?" asked Mary Dove.

"Yes, the same place."

"I thought I heard a girl saying she wouldn't be baptized there if she went to hell," Red said.

"She changed her mind. They decided they wouldn't let the sight of wickedness keep them away from the place the Lord had led them to."

"What time will they be there?" Red asked.

"The same as before," Brother Michael said. "They want to see you leaving then."

"We'll leave tonight," Red said. "I won't have that."

"They aim to watch and keep you here," the preacher said. "They want to see you go when they are gathered together. They think it's a church thing, and will be an example for the young people to remember."

"I don't care, Red, if we're together," Mary Dove said. "I don't care about them people. I hate to go off and leave our creatures, though, without nobody to take care of them."

"These good people that's running us off will take care of 'em, I imagine. With the owners gone, it won't be stealing if they take the chickens and livestock for theirselves."

"Red, they're good people," the preacher said softly. "They've been good to you, and yesterday you would have stood with them in all their beliefs. Don't forget that."

Red bowed over the table, supporting his head in his hands. "It's hard," he said.

"It's mighty hard," the preacher said. "Try not to judge them."

"Like they done me."

The preacher put a hand on Red's shoulder. "Yes, try," he said.

"I'll try," Red said.

"Then there's just one more thing," Brother Michael said, "and I'll leave you. The congregation took up a collection for me, and I have a little money. It's nowhere near what they're worth, but will you take it in exchange for the animals and improvements that you're leaving?"

Red looked up. "You aim to live here?"

"I'd like to, if I can. I don't expect I'll make a living preaching. I might file on some land."

"You could get all this anyway, without paying anything," Red said.

"I might. As you said, somebody would. But I thank God I can offer you some money for your journey."

"Yes, thank God," Red said. "It's a deal, Brother Michael." He stood and extended his hand.

The preacher shook hands with Red, then Mary Dove. Then he laid a purse on the table and, blessing them, was gone.

Red and Mary Dove came together and embraced. They stood silently supporting each other a long time and then, without saying what they must do, began gathering up a few things that they could take away with them.

Once Mary Dove sat down a few minutes and strummed the guitar. "I guess we couldn't take it," she said.

"Maybe some day we can write to Brother Michael," Red said, "and get him to send it to us."

"I was thinking we never would hear of him again," Mary Dove said, "or ever know what happened here at the dugout."

"It may not be that way," Red said.

"It may not be as bad as I thought," said Mary Dove. "It may be better than I ever thought our life could be."

At nightfall they went out to see about their animals.

"Them silly sheep," Mary Dove said. "Just think–before you come, Red, them sheep was nearly all my life to me."

"In a way," Red said, "it was them that led me to you."

"And now they wouldn't even know it if I tried to say goodbye."

She cried a little then, and Red held her close against him.

After they had finished their work they went back into the dugout and ate some milk and cold bread for their supper. They went early to bed, and found such comfort there in each other's arms that they slept through the long night without taking thought of the morrow.

17

It was the time of day when sunlight came down among the hills and sparkled in the unshadowed water that flowed out of Mary Dove's spring.

Mary Dove, wearing a bonnet pulled over her tightly braided hair and the loosest of her mother's dark print dresses, rode the gray mare and followed Red on Sangaree. They must go single file until they came up out of the creek bed, at the place where the bank turned gently sloping by the pool.

"Don't even look at them people," Red said to her.

"I will look," said Mary Dove. "I'm not afraid today, and I want to see them sisters clear and plain."

I will look, too, Red said to himself, for I am not ashamed.

All around the pool and ranged on the hill above it were the members of the newly gathered church. Along the rock shore, where Mary Dove had sat so many times, stood the sisters in their white summer dresses, with starched sleeves standing like wings, and in front of them Mr. Munden, with his shotgun lifted high.

No one made a sound or moved. They had not even frightened the dove away from his hackberry limb. He gave three clear grieving calls while Mary Dove watched him, and then flew away whimpering as Brother Michael moved out in front of the rest.

Brother Michael stayed as silent as the others but gave one flick of his hand, that might have been farewell, or might have been a sign to them to hasten. There was a smile on his face though–a smile of sadness and promise.

They passed the silent congregation and came onto the open bank where they would climb out of the creek bed. Red dropped back to ride beside Mary Dove, and reached and took her hand.

"Did you see the preacher smiling?" Mary Dove whispered.

"He wants us to think of the place we're going to, where people's laws is the same as God's."

Red squeezed her hand for an answer. He reckoned they might look a hundred years and never find that place, but he was glad that Mary Dove believed the promises.

Williamsburg Public Library
420 W. 2nd St.
Williamsburg, PA. 16693